WILLODEEN

WILLODEEN

KATHERINE APPLEGATE

Illustrations by
Charles Santoso

Feiwel and Friends
New York

A FEIWEL AND FRIENDS BOOK
An imprint of Macmillan Publishing Group, LLC
120 Broadway, New York, NY 10271
mackids.com

Our books may be purchased in bulk for promotional, educational, or
business use. Please contact your local bookseller or the Macmillan Corporate
and Premium Sales Department at (800) 221-7945 ext. 5442 or by email at
MacmillanSpecialMarkets@macmillan.com.

Library of Congress Control Number: 2021906928

First edition, 2021
Book design by Michelle Gengaro-Kokmen
Printed in the United States of America by LSC Communications,
Harrisonburg, Virginia
Feiwel and Friends logo designed by Filomena Tuosto

ISBN 978-1-250-14740-0 (hardcover)
10 9 8 7 6 5 4 3 2 1

For Mother Earth.
Thanks for putting up with us.

I have learned you are never too small to make a difference.

—*Greta Thunberg*

Part One

The little creature appears late one afternoon on an old carousel in the village of Perchance.

She is propped, dazed and damp as a newborn, on the saddle of a wooden unicorn.

She blinks, then blinks some more.

She makes a noise, a sort of squeaky growl.

Her breath comes and goes in tiny gasps and sighs. Her furry paws move when she tells them to. Her head turns this way and that.

She seems to be in fine condition.

But where is she? And more importantly, *why* is she?

She pats the neck of her lifeless steed. Perhaps she should wait here. Yes. That might be the best thing to do, under the circumstances. She does not know herself well yet. But she seems to be a patient sort. And patience, she suspects, might serve her well, might even save her life.

The creature has a maker, a boy with nimble fingers and a tender heart. He's spent hours weaving weeds and thistledown in the milky moonlight, spinning her into existence.

She has a friend as well, a girl with sharp eyes and a stubborn soul. And though the girl is young, she understands things that others do not.

The creature on her wooden horse knows none of this, not yet.

She does know, all at once and with great certainty, that she is quite alive, and quite alone.

Once upon a time, when stones were soft and stars were bits of dust, I loved a monster.

It seems forever ago, and perhaps it was, though things weren't really so different. True, magic was gentle then, and plentiful. But it's always there, if you know where to look. The moon, after all, still smiles from time to time, and the world still spins like a dancer through the skies.

In any case, the whens and wheres don't much matter.

The earth is old and we are not, and that is all you must remember.

TWO

I suppose I always loved strange beasts. Even as a wee child, I was drawn to them.

The scarier, the smellier, the uglier, the better.

Of course, I was kindly disposed toward all of earth's creatures. Birds and bats, toads and cats, slimy and scaly, noble and humble.

But I especially loved the unlovable ones. The ones folks called *pests*. *Vermin*. *Monsters*, even.

My favorites were called screechers. They

screamed at night like demented roosters, for no reason anyone could ever make out.

They were grumpy as tired toddlers. They were sloppy as hungry hogs.

And—I guess there's no nice way to put it—they stank to high heaven.

Get one riled, and he'd slap his big tail and give off a stench as ferocious as an outhouse in August.

And screechers were almost always riled.

That'll happen when people are constantly aiming arrows your way.

Screechers had needle-sharp teeth and dreadful claws. They had wild green-and-yellow eyes, two curlicue tusks, and more drool than a dog at dinner. They weren't big. About the size of a baby bear, I guess you'd say. Their bristly fur was plum-colored, and their tails looked like burnt flapjacks covered in quills.

I was the first to admit that screechers

weren't exactly charming. But I had a soft spot in my heart for them nevertheless.

I'm not sure why. Maybe I knew a thing or two about being unlovable myself. Maybe when the whole world was marching one way, some ornery part of me started shouting *Go the other way, Willodeen.*

You've just got to root for the underdog, don't you? And it sure seemed to me that screechers had always been the underdogs in nature's plan.

Although rooting for cute puppies would have been a whole lot easier.

Anyway. That's how it was.

It'd take someone a whole lot smarter than me to tell you why we love what we love.

CHAPTER
THREE

I saw my first screechers when I was six. I was out hunting for sunberries with my pa. I should have been at school, I s'pose. But my ma and pa had long since figured out that I was happier on my own. I'd tried attending a few times. But I felt awkward and uncertain around other children, and they seemed to feel the same way about me.

We didn't find a single berry. It hadn't

rained in forever and a day, and the bushes were shrunk and crumbly. We were about to give up when Pa whispered, "Willodeen!"

I followed his gaze. There she was, a ma screecher curled near a fallen tree, along with a tangle of five squirming, complaining babies.

Right off, she noticed us. She whacked her tail on the dirt, hard as could be.

Well, I knew what was coming next. Pa had warned me.

The smell is hard to describe. Put a hundred rotten eggs in your mind. Then add some scoops of dead fish and a splash of skunk spray. You'll have the general sense of things.

"Ain't her fault," Pa said, coughing and sniffling. "They rattle easy, poor creatures. And folks is always bothering them."

"But why?" I asked as I wiped stinging tears from my eyes.

"Claim they eat livestock. Kill pets, wild

game. Not a whit of truth to it. I seen 'em eat dilly bugs and the like. Mostly they live on peacock snails, grubs, worms." Pa rubbed his eyes. "'Course there's the matter of their . . . odor. Some say they scare off tourists." He laughed. "That much might be true, at least."

We stepped back from the nest, nice and easy, choking on the reek. Pa smiled in spite of it all.

"She's just doing what she's meant to do, my girl," he told me. "Caring for her own, best as she can. Like all us mas and pas."

You'd have thought we'd leave then, stinking as we did. But Pa pointed to a big rock nearby, and there we sat. Seemed we were far enough away for the ma screecher to calm herself.

Pa loved creatures, same as me, which is why we had so many roaming the nooks and crannies of our cottage and yard: goats and tree hares, chickens and dibby ducks, a peahen and an ancient river otter who could no longer swim. Our endless flow of cats and dogs had long since learned not to eat the other residents.

"See how gentle she is?" Pa said as the screecher nestled with her brood.

"I hear them at night sometimes," I said. "I wonder why they make that caterwaul noise, all screechy and harsh."

"Nobody knows for sure," said Pa. "Maybe they're like coyotes and wolves. Just singing to the stars."

"Maybe." I considered the possibility. "Too bad they can't carry a tune better."

Pa smiled. "Nature, Willodeen, knows more than we do, and she probably always will."

The ma screecher nudged one of the babies with her snout. "I wish people didn't hate them so," I said. "They were here first, when you think about it. It doesn't make sense."

Pa made a sad sighing sound, one he hardly ever made, and it startled me.

"If you're looking for folks to make sense, my girl," he said, "you may find yourself looking for a very long time indeed."

CHAPTER
FOUR

After washing our clothes with boiling water and lye soap, my ma finally admitted defeat and burned them in the hearth.

"Cursed screechers," she muttered at breakfast. "What in blazes do you two see in them? Can't eat 'em. Taste like they smell. Useless a critter as I ever met."

I glanced across the table at Pa and shared a smile. "Nature knows more than we do, Ma."

Pa winked. "And she probably always will."

My brother, Toby, who was two and a half, chose that moment to plop a bowl of porridge on his head. "Hat," he announced.

Ma gazed skyward and groaned. "Give me strength." She said that a lot. And then she laughed. She did that a lot, too.

She had a fine, wild laugh, my ma.

I never went berry hunting with Pa again.

A few weeks later, he was dead in the Great September Fire, along with my ma and little brother, like so many others in the village. Most of our animals died, too.

I survived, but just barely, and two neighbor women named Birdie and Mae took me in.

By the time I was ten, that particular fire had been forgotten by most, replaced by other dark days: mudslides, fevers, droughts, more fires.

It almost seemed the earth was mad at the lot of us.

Nature knows more than we do, Pa had said. But some days, that was hard to believe.

FIVE

I spent a long time in bed after the fire. I had some burns on my hands and the soles of my feet, but the real problem was all the smoke I'd had in my lungs, making deep breaths hard to come by.

While I recovered, Mae and Birdie gave me reading lessons and a book about dragons. My learning came quick, even if my healing did not. (We had a one-room school in the village, but it wasn't much to look at, and only a few children attended regularly. Most of us worked if we were big enough, or stayed out of the way if we were not.)

When I was better, and Mae and Birdie pronounced me ready to wander free, that's just what I did. Mostly I wanted to be alone. I felt safe in the hills. I was messy and clumsy. My elbows could always find the most breakable thing in a room. But walking in the woods, my body relaxed and I moved easily, like an animal that belonged there.

I liked keeping to myself. For as long as I could remember, people had always confounded me.

I'd given it careful thought and decided that most folks had a sort of clock in their heads. It told them when it was time to laugh at a joke. When to step closer for a whispered confidence. When to start a conversation, and when to say farewell.

My head seemed to be missing that invisible

clock. I was always just a bit late. Or a bit early. Never right on time. I was odd and wary, and that was just the way of things, like my gray eyes and my untamed hair, red and tangled as a wild rose vine.

I wasn't entirely alone, though. I had Duuzuu, my pet hummingbear. He'd survived the same fire I had, though his wings were so singed he would never fly properly again.

Mae and Birdie had found Duuzuu in the charred remains of a blue willow tree. They'd brought him to their cottage and nursed him back to health, same as me. I think they figured he'd bring me a bit of comfort during those bleak, endless days of recovery.

If you wanted to make an animal that's the opposite of a screecher, you might come close with a hummingbear. They're everything screechers are not.

Duuzuu was small enough to fit in the pocket of my coat, with room to spare for a biscuit. (Which he would no doubt eat.) His ears were round as coins. His fur reminded me of dandelion fuzz, ready for wishing. A pair of shiny wings sprouted from his back, and he had big eyes, always full of questions. His black, glossy tail curled in on itself like a fiddlehead fern in early spring. In his mouth, which seemed to rest in a permanent half smile, hid a long, sticky tongue that slurped up insects in an eyeblink.

Mostly, Duuzuu stayed in my pocket or perched on my shoulder. He could fly for a moment or two, but more often he trailed behind me in a sort of hopping run. At night, his delicate snores reminded me of a baby cricket, just learning to croon to the night.

Duuzuu seemed content, although I worried about him being without others of his own kind. One autumn, I even tried to introduce him to some other hummingbears. I set him down near a blue willow full of hummingbear nests and walked away, hard as it was to do.

Sadly, they wanted no part of him. They could fly, and he could not. And because hummingbears migrate over long distances each year, Duuzuu could never join them.

He was like me that way. Different. Solitary. Forever changed by fire.

In any case, he seemed to have settled on my company. I hoped I was enough.

CHAPTER
SIX

The annual arrival of the hummingbears was our village's claim to fame. They migrated down from the north in huge flocks, confusing the skies and crowding the clouds before landing on the blue willows in our valley. There they stayed until spring, when they flew back to their other home, an island hundreds of miles to the north.

It was breathtaking, seeing those animals clustered on the trees, their shimmering wings all fluttery. Why they'd chosen Perchance, no one was sure. It seemed to have something to do with the gentle winter climate and our stands of blue willows, the only trees where they'd nest.

Perchance was tucked in a valley surrounded by wooded hills like a baby in a green cradle. The River Essex ran through town, honey slow. Our blue willows loved the river. They craved water, clutching the banks with their knotty-fingered roots. And the hummingbears loved the willows.

It wasn't just their sweet faces and lovely cooing that made the hummingbears so irresistible. It was also their nests, made of glistening bubbles that absorbed sunlight and glowed all night, as if hundreds of miniature rainbows had gathered for a party.

No one knew quite how the hummingbears worked their nesting wizardry. They chewed willow leaves, somehow extracting the sap,

then blew tough-
walled bubbles.
The bubbles
adhered to
each other,
and to the
branches of
the willows,
with surprising
strength.

Most years, the
village held an Autumn Faire
to celebrate the arrival of the hummingbears,
and visitors came from near and far. When I
was seven, we'd had to call it off after a mud-
slide north of the village center. And when I
was nine, smoke from a fire two ridges over
had kept most visitors away.

But even without those problems, we'd all
noticed that fewer hummingbears were migrating to the village. Each autumn, the willows still

turned silvery-blue. The air still got a crisp-apple feel to it. And we still prepared for the onslaught of visitors. But something had changed.

It was worrisome, to say the least. Perchance depended on money from the tourists. Inns brimmed to overflowing with customers who bought food and ale and trinkets. A boy named Connor Burke made hummingbears out of willow and bark and sold them as souvenirs. Mae sold her thick knitted shawls. Nedwit Poole, the baker, created hummingbear-shaped pastries filled with berry jam.

The rest of the year, we made ends meet. We tended our garden plots. Some of us worked at the lumber mill. We fished in the river and hunted in the forest. A handful of men had jobs building tracks for the steam railway that skirted the village.

But the hummingbears and the Autumn Faire: that's what had always kept us afloat through the lean months.

Mostly I avoided the Faire, with its teeming crowds that made me feel like I was being smothered. So much noise! So much forced merrymaking!

Often I would see children there, ones I recognized from my rare visits to school. They moved in packs, like wild dogs. After they passed, I could hear them howling with laughter.

I wondered sometimes what it would be like to have a friend. To be so comfortable with myself that I could be comfortable with someone else, too.

But I was happy enough. I didn't need the complications and confusion that might come with friendship.

Usually, I could stand only a few minutes of the Faire before retreating to someplace quiet and safe. I loved seeing the hummingbears, of course. But it was the screechers that mattered most to me, and worried me more.

While we were seeing fewer and fewer hummingbears each fall, by the time I was nearly eleven, the screechers had all but disappeared.

I seemed to be one of the few people who'd noticed.

And I was quite sure I was the only one who cared.

SEVEN

While I was recovering from the fire, Mae and Birdie gave me a notebook, along with a sharp quill pen, a bottle of mirpetal ink, and several pencils. Each year after that, they gave me a fresh supply. Once I was better, I always kept a notebook and pencil with me in my waist-pouch. On my walks, I took notes. Before the fire, I'd just point out interesting things to Pa as I noticed them. But all by myself, I felt the need to keep a permanent record of what I observed.

I guess I'd come to understand that the world could change in a heartbeat.

I drew the till owls asking their one and only question: *Who? Who? Who?* I kept track of werebadger droppings and fresh fox dens. I sketched the buds peeking from the berry bushes. I counted the few blue willows in the hills. The more I watched and listened and stayed quiet and still, the more I understood the way of things.

But mostly I learned about screechers. I discovered what lazy nest builders they were, taking over the abandoned homes of others whenever they could. I watched them eating dandygrass and green grubs. I learned they almost never made their strange screechy noise when the sun was out.

And I counted. I've always had a gift for it. I like knowing the *how many* of things. At first it was hard to keep track. But eventually, I began to know the screechers as individuals. I learned to tell males from females. (The males had wider snouts and broader chests.) I recognized kin. Soon I had my favorite screechers, and I gave them names. Kerwin had a mere stump of a tail. Buddug had a missing right paw. Antlee was petite, with a stripe of white down her right side, but not her left.

I got to know the families, too, with their frolicking babes and grumpy grandparents, especially since some returned year after year. Screechers seemed to work hard at keeping their broods together. Older brothers and sisters often stood lookout near dens, and parents never let their babies wander far.

They had reason to be cautious. The village councillors had enacted a bounty on screechers after one ventured into a garbage pile during an Autumn Faire. A tourist happened upon him, the stench was bad for business, and that was that. Screechers were a nuisance, but nothing a well-aimed arrow couldn't fix.

Five pieces of copper for a screecher pelt! It infuriated me. Who could blame a curious animal for nosing around town with hope in his stomach?

Season after season, year after year, I kept counting. When I started, there were eighty-seven screechers. (I'm pretty sure, anyway. With that many, it was hard to keep them all straight.) The next year, I counted thirty-nine of them.

By the autumn I was about to turn eleven, I feared we might be down to one. Just one. Day after day I looked, and day after day I failed to find any more.

"Where is he?" I murmured to Duuzuu one afternoon. He was perched on my shoulder while I peered at an empty nest. It had been occupied by a family of four screechers the year before.

Duuzuu made a cooing noise. He always responded when I spoke. He had three distinct conversational noises. Sometimes it was a throaty purr. Sometimes it was a rising sound, like a question. Sometimes it was a soft, musical sigh. I was quite sure we were having a conversation. We just had no idea what we were saying to each other.

It was getting late. The sun was low, tired and flushed after a long day. The path was fir-shadowed. Here and there, sunbeams cut through the limbs like golden swords.

Near the top of the ridge, I knelt, searching for tracks in the dirt. It was cracked and hard—there'd been no rain for ages, it seemed—and I doubted I'd see anything much. But the screechers had sharp curved claws on each front foot, and sometimes those left marks.

Nothing, though I knew he'd been here yesterday. The only screecher I'd seen in two months. He was big and old, with a gray snout. I called him Sir Zurt. He was so old, I figured he deserved a knighthood, simply for surviving.

I sniffed the air. Was that smoke I smelled? Part of me was always on alert, waiting for the next fire. The next loss. Especially this time of year, when every day brought hot, dry winds.

I inhaled again. No smoke. But maybe, just maybe, I smelled screecher.

When they weren't frightened, screechers still had an odor about them. A good smell—at least I thought so—wild and earthy. I moved deeper into the trees and caught a glimpse of something.

There he was, curled up in a pile of debbir branches, his snout covered by a paw. A younger screecher would have noticed me approaching, but he probably couldn't hear or smell as well as he used to. He limped when he walked, like Mae and Birdie. I supposed screechers got the rheumatism, same as people.

I took a step closer. Sir Zurt opened one eye

and glared. He grumbled to let me know I'd
disturbed his nap.

I lowered my head and looked away. After
all my hours of watching, I'd learned that was
how to show I wasn't a threat. He relaxed a
bit, half closing his eyes.

I loved his eyebrow whiskers. Bushy and
silver-white. And his lashes, long and thick.

Behind me, a branch snapped. I heard foot-steps, movement.

Thwap.

The arrow hit with such force that the nest seemed to explode.

EIGHT

My heart lurched. "No!" I screamed, but my voice got lost in the cries of Sir Zurt and the lumbering steps of approaching hunters.

"Run!" I yelled. As if the old screecher could understand me.

I slipped Duuzuu into my coat pocket. "Hush," I said.

Sir Zurt was gone, but I saw a thin trail of blood leading into the trees. Quickly I covered

it with leaves. No need for the hunters to realize they'd hit their mark.

Another arrow sped past, landing in the abandoned nest. A third arrow struck a tree trunk
near my head.

I crouched low.
"Stop!" I cried. "He's
gone. Just *stop!*"

Through the branches,
I could make out two men
carrying bows, with quivers
of arrows strapped to their backs.
One man was short, dark-haired, and stocky.
The other was tall, with a thick gray beard and
large belly.

"Foolish child!" Gray Beard grumbled. "You
just cost me a pocketful o' coppers."

"Lucky we didn't hit you," said his companion.

I picked up the arrow near my feet. Its tip

was sharp as a screecher tail quill. The fletching reminded me of raven feathers.

"Give me that, you," said Gray Beard. His partner yanked on the arrow lodged in the tree trunk, but the shaft broke.

"Please. They don't deserve to be killed," I said.

Gray Beard plugged his nose. "Smell that?" he asked. "Ain't nothing worse 'an that stink."

I was so angry, I hadn't even noticed it. "They do that when they're afraid," I said. "They don't have arrows like you."

"Got sharp enough tusks and barbs on them tails," said the shorter man. "No need to stink up the world, too."

Gray Beard held out his hand. "Let's have it, then," he said, jerking his chin at the arrow I was still clutching.

My hands were trembling. I felt the tip, imagining the pain it could inflict. I'd handled many arrows, of course. My parents had taught me to hunt. I ate rabbit stew and chicken when I could, same as everyone else.

But to kill something for no reason, just because? Where was the sense in that?

"Hand it over, girl."

I didn't look at him. I avoided meeting people's eyes. It made my insides jittery.

Besides, I'd learned I didn't always like what I saw there.

"Now," he snapped.

But by then, I was already running down the hill, trailed by screams of rage.

CHAPTER
NINE

Nearly to the bottom of the hill, just out of sight of the village center, I glanced behind me. The hunters seemed to have given up.

My heart shouted at me to slow down. My eyes stung. I smelled awful. And yet it reminded me of the time I'd seen the screecher family while berry hunting with my father, that good day before everything had gone so wrong.

With a grunt, I tossed the arrow as far as I could into a patch of thick bushes.

Find *that*.

"Ow," said a bush.

I stopped cold.

A boy emerged. He held an armful of reeds and grasses in one hand and a lantern in the other. I recognized him as Connor, the boy who sold hummingbear souvenirs to the tourists each autumn.

He was a bit taller than me, with warm brown skin and a smile too large for his face. He squinted, then rubbed his nose. "You've been with your friends."

"My friends?" I frowned, because I didn't have any. Truth was, I'd *never* really had any.

"The screechers."

"You followed me?"

"Of course not. It's just . . . I've heard talk that you study them. And I go up that way sometimes. To get materials for my puzzlers."

"Puzzlers?"

Connor shrugged. "Things I make. I call

them that because I'm never sure how I'm going to put all the pieces together." He cocked his head. "Whose arrow was that?"

I looked at my feet. I did that a lot. I knew every last crease in my tired old shoes by heart.

"I think they killed him. An old screecher." My voice was low. "Two hunters. For no reason."

"For most people, money is always a reason."

"I really think he might have been the last. I haven't seen any other screechers in ages."

I made myself look at Connor. "Have you?"

He shook his head.

There was nothing more to say.

I took a few steps toward the village, then stopped. I needed to go back. To know for sure.

I spun on my heel and started a slow trudge back up the hill.

"You're going back?" Connor asked.

"I just want to know for sure. What if he's still alive and . . . suffering?"

"I'll go with you. I've got a lantern. And it'll be dark soon."

"I know these woods better than anyone." It was true. I knew the path by heart, knew all of Perchance cobblestone by cobblestone and weed by weed.

Connor set his grasses down by the side of the path. "You'd have better luck tomorrow, when it's light."

Tomorrow. I realized with a start that I'd be turning eleven tomorrow. I'd completely forgotten. "Tomorrow is my birthday," I blurted.

My cheeks burned. Why had I said that out loud?

I began walking faster, but Connor rushed to join me. "Here. You can borrow my lantern. Happy birthday."

I looked up at the ridge. The forest had

changed from a collection of trees to a dark, formless mass. He was right about needing light.

Mae and Birdie had been right, too. They'd urged me to take a lantern, but I'd refused.

"Stubborn as the day is long," said Birdie, who was every bit as stubborn as I was.

"Sometimes it's better to bend than break," said Mae. She was more inclined toward gentle persuasion, not that it worked on me.

I didn't want Connor's lantern. It would just mean having to return it to him later. And I certainly didn't want his company.

But I did want light.

Right on cue, Duuzuu poked his head out of my pocket and cooed.

"Hello there," said Connor. He held out his hand, and, to my annoyance, Duuzuu clambered out of my pocket, up Connor's arm, and onto his shoulder.

"I love hummingbears," Connor said.

"They're amazing. Is this the one that was hurt in the fire?"

I nodded, surprised he'd heard about Duu-zuu. But in Perchance, people seemed to know everything about everybody.

Duuzuu cooed again.

"Fine," I said to Connor. "You can come. What about your grasses and reeds?"

"They're not going anywhere."

I walked as quickly as I could, eyes peeled for any sign of the hunters, with Connor and Duuzuu at my side.

The moon was caught behind clouds, and the forest wore the night like a thick cloak. I had to admit I was glad for the yellow glow of Connor's lantern.

Near the top of the ridge, I paused and angled into the trees.

It wasn't hard to find him.

I knew he was dead before I even got there.

His eyes stared at nothing. His white snout was covered in blood.

Duuzuu made his questioning noise, and Connor reached up to stroke him between the ears.

I gathered leaves and pine needles, covering the body as best as I could. It wasn't a proper burial, but the dirt was too hard for much else.

I knew the old screecher would have died soon, anyway. I also knew that before long other animals—surrbears, maybe, or wolves—would find his body and use what they could of it. That was nature's way.

We didn't talk as we headed back down. But in my head, a sad refrain repeated with each footfall: *He was the last, the last, the last.*

CHAPTER
TEN

Near the bottom of the hill, Connor gathered up his materials. "I can walk you home if you'd like," he offered.

"No need." I sounded rude to my own ears, so I added, "Thank you for going with me to . . . you know."

Connor's dark eyes caught the lantern light. "Have you ever heard one call at night? A screecher, I mean?"

"Plenty. Not in a long time, though."

"I've always wondered what they're trying to say."

"Me too. I'm starting to think we'll never know."

"Well," said Connor. "Good night, then."

"Wait." I held out my arm. "Come on, Duuzuu."

Duuzuu hesitated, then hopped over to my shoulder obediently. "I guess he likes you," I said, somehow feeling a bit betrayed.

Connor turned right, and I headed toward the village center. The cottage was on the other side of town.

Near the river, workers had erected a wooden platform for the Autumn Faire. The windows of the taverns glowed with flickering candlelight, but I didn't see many people inside.

Already, musicians, jugglers, and a handful of tourists had made their way into town. Still, things felt off. There was a quiet unease about the place.

Along the riverbank, torches burned in preparation for the Faire, but I saw no hummingbears. Usually by now the trees would be glimmering with a few early arrivals and fresh nests.

I made my way down the riverwalk, the long path bordering the waterfront, trying to ignore the villagers who plugged their noses as they passed.

"Take a dip in the river! You're stinkin' up the place!" an old woman grumbled.

Three girls about my age approached, arms linked. I knew them from my brief visits to school, and of course, I'd seen them around the village. Violet, Poppy, and Primrose. I'd nicknamed them the "flower friends." I never saw one without the other two nearby.

"What's that I smell?" Poppy asked, loud enough to be sure I heard.

"That's the screecher girl," Primrose said as they walked past me.

Normally I would have cowered, but I was mad. And anger made me louder.

"It's my new perfume!" I yelled to their backs. "Do you like it?"

Their laughter reminded me of cawing crows.

I didn't care one whit about those girls. They didn't matter.

The last. The last. The last.

Beside me, the blue willows swayed in the breeze. Their long leaves had already turned silver on one side and deep blue on the other. They were mesmerizing in their fall colors. But without the hummingbears and their shimmering nests, the trees seemed lonely and unfinished.

Near the edge of the village, I took a left. The cottage was close enough to see.

I couldn't bring myself to call it home, exactly. Seemed I could never use that word without thinking of my old home, my ma, my pa, my brother, our animals. The chipped teapot with the yellow flowers painted on the side. The wooden rocker where Pa sat and smoked his pipe by the fire. My sagging bed with its carving of a robin in the headboard.

All gone. All gone, but a shard of Ma's teapot that I'd found in the charred remains of my home.

My old home.

No matter. It was over. It was done. Pain was best packed away. Covered up. The way I'd tried to cover Sir Zurt.

I was good, it seemed, at burying things.

The cottage was warm and smelled of pea soup.

Mae was dozing by the fire. Birdie was stirring a black pot. "Well, look who's decided to grace us with her company," she said. She wrinkled her nose. "So you found one, I see. Or should I say 'I smell'?"

To my shock, I began to cry. Hard, gasping sobs. The kind I hated, because it meant I'd lost control.

"Willodeen?" said Mae, getting slowly to her feet. "What's wrong, lamb?"

"They killed him," I said. "Sir Zurt."

I didn't have to say any more. Mae and Birdie surrounded me in a tight embrace and let me sob away.

And though I knew they weren't really my family, and I knew the cottage wasn't really my home, it was good to be held, to listen to the fire crackle and the soup in the kettle gently simmer.

ELEVEN

Mae and Birdie were impossibly old and crotchety. There wasn't any job they hadn't done during their long lives, it seemed, including working as healers, and their cottage was filled to the brim with potions and herbs, glass bottles and mortars and pestles. But their favorite work by far had been acting in a traveling theater troupe. A day never went by without one of them breaking into song, reciting a sonnet, or dancing a jig. It was the price I had to pay, Birdie said, for living with two former thespians.

I owed them everything, and I knew it. They'd spent many sleepless nights tending to me after the fire. And they'd welcomed me like I was kin. I did my best to show my gratitude. I weeded our garden, sold eggs from our coop, took odd jobs when I could find them, did every chore they asked of me, and then some.

Still, I tried hard not to let myself care for them too much. They made it easier than it might have been. They could be surly as . . . well, as screechers. Mae was round and red-cheeked. Birdie was broomstick-thin, taller than any woman I'd ever met, and even most men. They both had mounds of white hair piled in flat puffs atop their heads like melting snowballs.

People called them witches. Whispered about them. *No husbands. No children. Strange birds.* It made me want to protect them. But truth be told, Mae and Birdie didn't seem to need protecting. They'd been together, they said, since before the dawn of time. And despite their occasional squabbles, it was clear as could be that they loved each other dearly.

After a supper of hot soup and crusty bread, I did my evening chores and headed straight to bed. My room was cramped—it had been a pantry before my arrival—but it was cozy and had a window, and that was all I needed.

That night, the moon hid beyond clouds, and sleep hid from me.

Duuzuu snored peacefully on my pillow. Everything about him was curled. He slept in a tight ball, his tail looped, wings hugging his round body.

How did he sleep so soundly? After all these years, I still woke up dreaming of fires, of screams, of helplessness. Sometimes, I'd be the one screaming out loud, and Birdie and Mae would come running in to soothe me.

Duuzuu had been through the same fire I had. Why didn't he have bad dreams? Did animals remember things the same way we did? Or did the world just exist from moment to moment for them?

I closed my eyes. I saw Sir Zurt lying on the forest floor.

I opened my eyes. Ceiling. Clouds. Quilt.

Eyes closed again. I saw two men grabbing my hands and pulling me through a broken window. I heard the fire growl like a living thing, heard myself yelling *Pa! Ma! Toby!* until my throat knotted and I lost consciousness.

Eyes open. Duuzuu. My worn and dusty shoes. My notebooks.

I lit my lantern, reached for a notebook, and thumbed through its pages. Sometimes that calmed me. Over time, I'd learned ways to trick myself into slumber.

I glanced over the pages. It had been two months since I'd seen any screecher but Sir Zurt.

I skimmed some more. It had been eleven months since I'd heard a screecher call out at night.

That was almost a year ago, right after I'd turned ten.

Tomorrow I would be eleven. Not that I felt there was much to celebrate. I knew there would be no gifts. We hadn't the coins to spare for such things.

I closed my eyes and tried to recall my last birthday with my family. Pa and Ma had just finished building our home. It was made of logs and mud and time, mostly. A simple dwelling, but they were proud of it. I'd even helped a bit. Or at least my parents had pretended to let me help.

All that work and sweat. That building and dreaming. Gone in a flash, in a frenzy of flames.

What was the point in making things, if they only came to ashes?

All too often, I'd drift off, only to wake from nightmares about the fire that had killed my family. I'd be bathed in sweat, screaming for help, gulping for air.

It happened so often, I almost expected it.

It wasn't so bad, really. Mae and Birdie always ran to comfort me. And sometimes I even managed to fall back into an uneasy slumber.

That night was different. Instead of flames and death, I dreamed I heard a screecher calling.

I woke, startled and hoping, for a moment, anyway.

But no.

The moon was still hiding. And the world was still quiet.

Part Two

The creature takes in her new world.

Things to touch, to smell, to taste. Breezes filled with possibilities.

She glances behind her. A long, flat, bristly part is attached to her rear.

She extends her paws. Sharp, curved things appear. She startles. They are scary to see. But apparently, they belong to her, too.

She tries to stand on the wooden saddle of her quiet horse.

She plops to the ground but lands unhurt.

Blink. Blink. If she closes her eyes, the world goes away. If she opens them, it's all there again, color and light and shadow.

She takes a step. It's hard to move four feet at the same time. Maybe two and two will work?

She walks back and forth, trying possibilities. Right front, left back. Left front, right back.

Oomph. She topples over onto her snout.

Shouldn't someone be explaining the world to her?

Shouldn't there be others nearby, for warmth, for comfort?

She sees a tree with blue-and-silver leaves, long and twirly.

She's drawn to it, though she doesn't know why. It means something. Something good.

Something necessary.

She waddles over to the knotty base of the tree and sits.

Already she is tired. Becoming is hard work.

But she cannot close her eyes. The world is a dangerous place. Somehow she knows that much, at least.

TWELVE

Mae and Birdie were still snoring when I woke early the next morning. I dressed quick as I could—mornings could be chilly, now that autumn had arrived—then threw on my coat. Lazy Duuzuu, always the last to awaken, still dozed.

On the table sat a small round cake, listing to one side, with a squat candle in its center. It was kind of Mae and Birdie to remember my birthday, when I'd almost for-gotten it myself. The cake had taken time and thought, and sugar we didn't have leave to waste.

I rushed outside and grabbed three logs from the woodpile near the porch. My breath made clouds. On the way back, I noticed something sitting on the old rocker near the door.

I peered closer. It looked like one of the cre-ations I'd seen Connor sell at the Faire. What had he called them? His "puzzlers"?

I dropped my logs. The sculpture was made of bits and pieces of nature. Bark and reeds, mud and leaves, twigs and stones. Spiderwebs and glistening drops of tree sap seemed to be holding it all together.

But it wasn't a hummingbear. No, this could only be one thing, and it was perfect in every detail, right down to the twisty tusks made of spiraling reeds. The spiny, flat tail of layered pine needle quills. The green haynut slivers for eyes.

It was a screecher.

I looked right and left. Was Connor still nearby? When had he left this? It had a dusting of frost on it, so perhaps it had been waiting here for a while.

I left the logs behind and carried the sculpture inside. Gently, I set it on the table. Then I pulled up a chair and stared.

He had it all right, every last detail. How could he remember with such precision? And how did he create such beauty?

For it *was* beautiful, even though it was a screecher.

But why had he made it?

I'd never been the kind of person to make things. I lacked the patience. And, to be honest, the talent.

I supposed there was some sense in creating practical things. The way Mae knitted shawls to fight the winter chill. The way Ma had cooked meat pies for supper. The way Pa had made a henhouse out of discarded lumber.

The way we'd made a home together.

A home that was no more.

But this? This served no purpose. And yet . . . and yet it made me smile. I stroked the creature's nose.

I might never see another screecher. But at least I'd have this.

It felt wrong somehow, being pleased by a gift from a virtual stranger. I didn't like the feeling. It made me beholden. Needy.

Connor didn't even know me. Not really.

I ran my fingers over the bow tied around the beast's neck, over its frightening claws, its dangerous tail.

I hadn't a clue why Connor had left this for me. I didn't understand my own feelings most days. I couldn't begin to figure out why other people did the things they did.

Maybe it didn't matter.

I wanted it. I needed it to be mine.

And it was.

THIRTEEN

We decided to have cake for breakfast. Mae and Birdie were like that, not much for the usual polite rules of home and hearth. Which suited me fine.

They were both delighted by the screecher Connor had made. Mae held it up to the light, examining it from every angle. "I still can't get over the details on this thing," she marveled.

"Be sure you say thank you when you see

Connor next," Birdie reminded me. "That took a great deal of work. And kindness."

"I will," I said, although secretly I hoped I wouldn't run into Connor anytime soon. I had a hard enough time just saying "hello" and "goodbye" to people.

"Make a wish," Mae instructed as she lit the candle. Duuzuu, who'd finally roused himself, half hopped, half flew onto the table, eyeing the cake hopefully.

I looked at Birdie and Mae, at their expectant, kind faces, lined by life.

"Thank you," I said, "for making it. It's very nice."

"No, it isn't," said Birdie. "It looks like a dying toadstool." She lifted her bony shoulders. "What can I say? Baking bores me to tears. All that work, and before you know it, it's in one end and out the other."

"I'm sure it's wonderful." Mae patted my

back. "Go on, now. Wish for something. It's good for the soul."

What did I want? I tried not to long for things. Even if you got what you wanted, it could be snatched away in an instant.

Out of nowhere, I thought of Sir Zurt, lying in his blanket of leaves, and fresh tears came. Bothersome eyes. I hated the way they spouted water so easily, betraying me at every turn.

"Oh, dear me," said Mae. "The waterfall has returned." She dabbed at my cheeks with her handkerchief.

"I'm not sad, exactly." I sniffled. "I'm mad. These are mad tears." Somehow that seemed more acceptable.

"Angry tears have magic in them," said Birdie.

I rolled my eyes.

"She's right," said Mae. "There's great power in tears born of anger."

Mae and Birdie were always saying things like that.

"I've half a mind to bottle those up," said Birdie. She gave a brief smile. Birdie's smiles were often uncertain, more like fickle frowns. "I'll just grab an empty vial. Could you manage some more?"

"Now, Birdie, don't be greedy." Mae dipped a finger into the icing on the cake and popped it into her mouth. "Those tears belong to Willodeen, and she may need them."

"What's the point in being mad?" I crossed my arms over my chest. "No one cares what I think. I'm just . . . just an eleven-year-old child." I'd had to catch myself before saying "ten."

"You're an eleven-year-old *person*," Mae corrected.

"Well, I'm not exactly a grown-up."

"Piffle," said Mae.

"I second her piffle," said Birdie. "Grown-ups are just boring former children."

71

Mae tried to scoop off another bit of icing, and Birdie sent her a warning look.

"But grown-ups," I persisted, "run the world."

"Well, we're not exactly doing a first-rate job of it, are we?" said Mae.

Birdie squeezed my hand. "Don't stop being angry, Willodeen. It's part of who you are. You see the world differently. You care. That's a gift."

"It sure doesn't feel like a gift." It was my turn to poke at the icing. "Why is everything so complicated?"

"Because we are humans, and humans are notoriously difficult," said Mae.

She winked at Birdie. "Ourselves included."

Birdie leveled a finger at me. "Yes, Willodeen. Even you."

They were humoring me, I knew. Trying to nudge me out of my bad mood.

"And now, my dear," said Mae, "if you don't make a wish, I shall make one for you. My stomach is grumbling, and the candle's down to a nub."

I couldn't think of a single wish. But Mae was clearly hungry.

I closed my eyes and took a deep breath, just as one last, annoying tear made a path down my cheek. *If only angry tears really did hold magic*, I thought.

It was as close to a wish as I could come. I blew out the candle, and we began eating, with Duuzuu's enthusiastic help.

FOURTEEN

We finished every last morsel of cake. Duu-zuu was so full, he promptly went back to sleep on my pillow, his belly swollen.

I headed outside to feed the animals and gather eggs. To my shock, there was Connor, leaning over the fence to pat Rufus, our black-bellied goat. "My next puzzler is going to have goat eyes," he said. "I love how strange they are. The pupils!"

"Why are you here?" I asked, and then I realized how it must have sounded. "I . . . thank you for the, um, gift."

"Could you tell what it was?"

I couldn't help laughing. "Could I *tell*? It was perfect! You got every detail right."

Connor seemed relieved. "Oh, good. I was in a hurry. I made it last night. I wasn't sure about the tail."

"Last night?" I repeated. "You made that in one night?"

"You said today was your birthday, and I thought . . ." He trailed off.

"It's, well, it's really wonderful."

I moved past him, grabbed a wicker basket, and leaned into the coop. The hens and dibby ducks clucked with annoyance as I gathered their smooth, warm eggs.

"Actually, I'm here because last night I remembered a blue willow grove near the northwest ridge," Connor said as I emerged from the coop. "Just a few trees, hidden by taller firs. Do you know it?"

"No," I said, frowning. I'd thought I knew every inch of the hills around Perchance.

"Well, there was an abandoned den there. Fox, maybe? Didn't seem like it had been used in a while. But since it was near those willows, and sometimes I've seen screechers digging around their roots . . ." He paused. "I thought maybe we could take a look."

I would certainly check. But I didn't like the "we" part.

"Doubt there's anything there," I said. "I've spent months searching all around here."

I glanced down at my basket of eggs. The striped dibby duck eggs were my favorites. "Well, then." I turned back toward the cottage. "Thank you again."

To my annoyance, instead of leaving, Connor followed me. I'd said a proper thank-you.

Shouldn't he go now? This proved that accepting a gift just led to trouble.

I opened the cottage door, and Mae was there, sweeping. "Well," she said, "hello!"

She looked at me expectantly, so I said, "Mae, this is Connor Burke. He made the screecher."

"The artist!" she exclaimed.

"Oh, it's not art, really," Connor said with a shy smile. "It's just a thing I like to do. Keeps my hands busy."

"Of course it's art. You created it. And did you enjoy making it?"

Connor rubbed his chin. "Well, yes. I guess I did."

Mae set aside her broom and brushed her hands on her skirt. "Well, there you go, then. Art! Come in, come in!"

Mae ushered Connor inside, and I followed reluctantly. "Birdie!" she called. "It's the screecher artist!"

I took my time placing the eggs I'd gathered into a large bowl. I didn't like having Connor in the cottage. It was my territory, even if it wasn't my true home. In that way, I was like any smart wild animal.

"What else do you do, when you're not making screechers?" asked Birdie, who was busy preparing a liniment rub for her rheumatism.

"I like to write stories and poems now and then. And sketch."

"A poet and an artist!" Birdie exclaimed. "The world could use more of you."

"Amen to that," said Mae.

And I could use less of you, I thought. I made a loud throat-clearing noise.

"Well," Connor said, "I suppose I should go. There's a village council meeting, and Father likes me to attend. He's one of the councillors. He says it's good practice."

"Good practice for what?" Birdie asked as she ground rosemary leaves with a pestle.

Connor shook his head. "Becoming him, I suppose. He works over at the lumber mill."

"Ahh," said Mae. "And is that your plan as well?"

"Mae," Birdie chided. "You're doing it again."

Mae pressed her palm to her chest, feigning offense. "*Moi?* Doing what?"

"Poking and prodding where you've no business."

"That's all right," Connor said with a good-natured wave of his hand. "I don't really have a plan, not yet. There's not much of a future in making puzzlers and poems, I expect."

"In my experience—in *our* experience," Mae said, casting a fond glance at Birdie, "it's best for all concerned if you simply go ahead and be what you are meant to be. Saves valuable time."

I cleared my throat again. I was not a person given to subtlety.

"Well, happy birthday, Willodeen," Connor said, turning toward the door.

"Thank you again, Connor," I said.

Relieved to see him leaving, I managed what I hoped was a grateful smile, but just then, Birdie slammed her palm on the table with such force that I jumped. "Here's a thought!" she cried, waving her pestle in the air. "Why don't you attend the council meeting with Connor?"

I looked over my shoulder, but apparently, she was talking to me.

She might as well have said, "Why don't you borrow a pair of wings and fly to the moon?"

FIFTEEN

"Me?" I said, sending her a dark look.

"Of course you," Birdie said. "Speak your mind. Tell them how you feel about the bounty on the screechers. Get it off your chest." She nodded and threw out her arms dramatically. "Unburden!"

"Proclaim!" Mae added.

I sneaked a glance at Connor, who seemed to think this was a wonderful idea.

My throat clenched at the very thought. I

81

hated speaking up in public. I barely spoke up in the safety of the cottage. "I couldn't!" I protested. "Besides . . . nobody would listen to me."

"Probably not," Birdie admitted. "At least, not at first."

I groaned. "Then why bother?"

"Because these things take time," said Birdie.

Mae nodded. "Lots of time. Change doesn't happen overnight, my dear."

"Well, if it's such a good idea to speak up, why don't you two ever go to council meetings?" I asked.

Mae glanced at Birdie. "She has a point, Bird."

"She does indeed." Birdie pursed her lips. "I suppose we don't attend because we're old."

"And tired," Mae offered.

Birdie nodded. "And lazy."

"Don't forget cynical," said Mae. "Also jaded."

"But you, Willodeen, are none of those

things." Birdie made a shooing motion with her hands. "Off with you, then."

"No!" The word practically exploded from my lips. "I mean . . . I have work to do. The animals. And we need more wood. And—"

"You know there's no point in arguing with us," Birdie said. "Best be on your way, Willodeen. We'll take care of things."

I narrowed my eyes. When they started in on me like this, I usually lost. But they had to know I'd never speak up at the meeting. I wondered if they were trying to get me to spend time with Connor, in the hope I'd make a friend at long last.

Connor held open the door, as if we'd been planning an outing all along.

"Hurry now," Birdie snapped. "You're letting in the chill. Be off, girl. Do something useful with all that anger."

Before I knew 'it, I was standing on the porch with Connor.

"Wait," I said, panicking.

I rushed back inside. Was it rude to slam the door in someone's face?

The disappointed looks from Mae and Birdie told me the answer.

"I, uh, forgot this," I said, by way of an excuse. I grabbed the puzzler and wrapped it in a napkin.

I decided to try one last time. "It's my birthday," I said, angling for sympathy. "This is not how I wanted to spend it."

"This is a perfect way to spend it," said Mae. "Now scoot. Begone."

"Fine," I muttered.

"Remember," Birdie called, "there's magic in your anger."

I closed the door behind me, loudly. "Piffle," I muttered.

Connor was standing by the front gate. "Did you just say 'piffle'?"

"No," I lied.

"I figured you went back to get Duuzuu."

"He's asleep," I said. "I wanted to get this." I held up the screecher in its napkin wrapping, and the pleased look on Connor's face almost made me forget how little I wanted to be there.

"It probably needs to dry some more," he said. "If anything breaks, I can fix it, though."

"I'll be careful." Gently I slipped it into my pocket, and off we went.

When I glanced over my shoulder, I saw Mae and Birdie through the window, looking far too pleased with themselves.

CHAPTER

SIXTEEN

We walked to the center of town without saying a word. To my relief, things weren't as
awkward as I'd expected. Still, I felt there was
something more I should be doing. Talking?
Was that it?

Should I remark on the weather? The dec-
orations for the Faire? Sometimes I felt like
everyone in the village had read the same book
about friendship, then tossed it in the river
before I could read it.

In any case, it didn't matter. We simply walked. The air was fresh, with the sharp edge you felt only in autumn, though we didn't see a single hummingbear when we passed the blue willows at the river's edge.

It was Connor who broke the silence. "Do you think what I do . . . making the puzzlers, I mean. Do you think it's—"

"Odd?" I suggested.

Connor scratched the back of his head. "Yes, that'll do. I suppose. Odd."

"Yes," I said. I didn't mean it unkindly. It was the simple truth. People were often so quick to avoid the honest answer to a question.

"A lot of people at school would say the same thing." He gave a short laugh. "Of course, look at you." His voice was gently teasing. "You're obsessed with the most hideous beasts in the land, after all."

"So?" My pa had taught me that *"So?"* was

a fine response to almost any insult. And it was remotely possible that I'd been insulted. "Birdie and Mae say being different is a useful thing."

"Hmm." Connor considered the idea. "My father says being different makes life more difficult."

I watched the leaves on the blue willows twirl, silver to blue, blue to silver. "I guess both things could be true," I said at last.

The village hall was a squat building, nothing much to look at. It had been rebuilt after a fire consumed the original hall. The same fire that had killed my family.

At the front steps, Connor warned, "Prepare yourself."

"For what?"

"Silly debates. Endless bluster. Arguments over nothing."

"Do you go to all these meetings?"

"Most of them. My father thinks it's a good way for me to learn about the world. Sometimes I nap when no one is looking. Or sketch. Or write stories."

Connor started up the stairs, but I hesitated. "I think I'll wait here," I said. "To be honest, I really don't want to do this."

"Me neither. But I promise it's not so bad. Come on." He jerked his head toward the door. "I could use the company."

I took a step. Another. One of my shoelaces was loose. I stopped to retie it.

Still Connor waited.

"I don't much like crowds," I said to my shoe. My hands were sweating. My face was hot.

"Who does?" Connor laughed. "Really, I promise there's nothing to be afraid of, Willodeen."

Well, *that* set me off.

Yes, I was afraid. But there was no way anyone else needed to know.

I sprinted up the stairs and left Connor in my wake.

CHAPTER

SEVENTEEN

The interior was stuffy and crowded. High round windows provided circles of light. Most people sat on benches. Pipe smoke twirled while voices rose and fell.

"I usually sit over there," Connor said, pointing to a bench near the right side.

In the front of the room, seated at a long, low table, were five men and one woman. Connor waved, and a man gave a curt nod. His father, no doubt. They had the same sharp-edged jaw and lanky build. But Mr. Burke had a stern look about him that made me want to lower my gaze.

I recognized the woman at the table as Miss Rossit, the only teacher at our one-room school. She was short and sturdy, with straw-colored hair tied in a braid. This time of year, there was no school, as everyone had to pitch in to help with the Faire. (Although, like many village children, I hadn't attended in much longer. Birdie and Mae left such things up to me, and I had no desire to spend time indoors with others when I could be roaming the hills on my own. I doubted I was missing anything.)

As we settled, a gavel pounded, and the sound echoed in the rafters. "The council meeting will now commence," announced the chair, an older gentleman with wild white hair and an immense mustache.

"That's Thaddeus Vilner," Connor whispered as he pulled a journal and a sharp pencil from his coat pocket. "My father says he has terrible breath."

I tried to hide my smile.

"The agenda for today," said Thaddeus, "is one thing only, as we all well know. Our livelihoods are in jeopardy, and our winter may be bleak indeed, unless we determine what has happened to the hummingbears we all love. This year things appear to be worse than ever." He scanned the room. "Has anyone seen a hummingbear migrate in yet?"

Miss Rossit held up her hand. "A fortnight ago I saw two hummingbears. They were flying south. I watched them pass right over the riverfront willows and keep going."

Thaddeus grimaced. "Anyone else?"

The crowd was silent, but not for long. As Connor had promised, a great deal of talking followed, and not all of it about hummingbears.

The villagers' words poured out with such

force I feared I might drown in them. I hadn't heard this much talk in the past five years combined. It made me dizzy and breathless. At one point, I decided I needed some fresh air. I moved to stand, but Connor took my arm and pointed to a sketch he'd been working on. It was Duuzuu, soaring through the clouds.

It was a good likeness, although it made me wistful, knowing Duuzuu would never fly like that again. Smiling, I settled back on our bench and tried to collect myself. I closed my eyes and took long breaths, and as I listened I began to hear not just the cascade of words, but the pain behind them.

Every villager's statement held the same feeling: fear. Mostly, they talked about the hummingbears. What if the migrations ceased altogether? How could people feed their children without the money from tourists?

But there were other worries, too. What if another fire came this year? The hot autumn winds, the ones we called "Dragon Sighs," were blowing with more force than in years past. Garden harvests had been disappointing, too. How could we plant when we had no idea whether or not it was going to rain?

I found myself counting the worries the way I counted screechers. Seven villagers mentioned the lack of rain. Eleven talked about fire. Twenty-two wondered where the hummingbears were going. Six talked about their dying crops. Four mentioned how the mill upriver had disrupted fishing. Two worried about the railway cutting through the forest surrounding Perchance.

I felt a bit sorry for all the adults. How hard it must be to worry all the time about your children and their future!

I heard fear. And impatience. And a great deal of frustration. The problem, it seemed to me, was that the villagers couldn't decide where to direct their anger. Several blamed the councillors, although it wasn't exactly clear what they'd done wrong. Others said we'd angered the heavens. A few even blamed nature herself for letting us down.

And one gruff gentleman carrying a walking stick blamed plain old bad luck.

On that, at least, everyone seemed to agree.

They agreed far less on what to do. Waiting and hoping, on the one hand, or raging and cursing, on the other, seemed to be the two favored approaches. But there was a great deal of squabbling, blaming, and back-and-forthing.

Grown-ups seemed to be quite good at that.

One of the last men to speak came from the back of the room, but I recognized his thick gray beard instantly.

"Otwel Borwan here," he said.

"You have the floor, Mr. Borwan," said Thaddeus.

"I've got me an idea. Seems there's plenty of coin in the village coffers—"

"Actually," Mr. Burke interrupted, "that's not the case," but Otwel forged ahead. "There's money enough," he said. "Why not raise the bounty on pests? Give us something to spend, at least while we wait things out. A lot of us are down to our last coppers."

A man near the front leapt up. "If there's money to be had, we should spend it on mending Main Street."

"How about repairs to the school?" someone else called. Others chimed in with more suggestions: a new roof for the village hall, food for families whose crops had failed, a fresh planting of blue willows to attract more hummingbears.

"Ahem," Otwel said. "Pretty sure I'm the one who's doin' the talkin' at the moment?"

"Go ahead, Mr. Borwan. You were saying something about pests?" said Miss Rossit. She had a skeptical gaze I appreciated.

"Screechers and the like. Rats and mice,

too." He shrugged. "How about fair wages to clean up the village? It'd help out a few of us, at any rate."

At the word "screechers," my pulse quickened. I felt words forming even as I tried to bottle them up.

"I'd argue that screechers are the least of our problems," said Thaddeus. "Hardly any left to speak of."

"And whose fault is that?" someone cried.

And it seemed I was that someone.

CHAPTER

EIGHTEEN

Some part of myself, watching the following moments unfold, was shocked. I could see my red face, my frazzled hair, my clenched fists. I could see the crowd, too, aghast at this interruption from a mere child.

"You!" Otwel shouted. "You're the screecher girl! The one who stole my arrow from me. I thought the place reeked. Shoulda known."

Thaddeus held up his palm. "We will have order in this meeting."

But my words kept coming, gushing forth. "We don't have any screechers because of that stupid bounty," I yelled. "And they were harming no one. Why waste your money on killing animals who don't need killing?"

"We're not here to discuss the lack of screechers," said Mr. Burke in a calm voice. "We're here to discuss the lack of humming-bears. We need them. We certainly do not need more screechers."

"Ain't nobody needs screechers," Otwel said, and the crowd snickered.

"I'm just saying . . ." Was I still standing? Was I still speaking? I glanced at the crowd and briefly considered fainting. So many faces, all staring at me.

Connor's eyes were wide, but he made a nod of encouragement.

"I'm just saying—" I began again, then faded.

"You oughta be sayin' ya plan on replacing that arrow ya stole," Otwel muttered.

"In light of this digression, perhaps I should remind us all," said Thaddeus, "that we are assembled here to discuss why the humming-bears are failing to return."

Apparently, I wasn't done.

"Maybe . . . maybe it's us," I said, surprised to learn I still had words left to speak. "We're the ones who keep changing things." My father's voice whispered in my head. "Truth is, nature knows more than we do."

"Sit down, young lady," said Thaddeus. "We've heard quite enough from you."

That ornery part of me, the one always urging *Go the other way, Willodeen*, reared up, ready for a fight.

I felt the screecher sculpture in my pocket. Anger boiled in my chest.

"These animals . . . screechers . . . they're as much a part of things as you and me." I took a steadying breath. "Look, I don't know why the hummingbears are gone. I don't know why the world is changing so fast and so wrong. But I do know that nature's a complicated thing. It's like . . . it's like, I don't know, like knitting a sweater. You pull one string too hard, and the whole thing starts unraveling. I'm just saying let's not lose things before we get the chance to understand them. Screechers included."

Silence.

Murmurs.

Laughter.

It was time to leave. I walked toward the door, holding my head high, though I stumbled more than once.

As I reached for the handle, I turned to see if Connor might be following me, but he was still seated, avoiding the stern glare of his father.

I slammed the door, for the second time that day.

This time I hoped it was rude.

NINETEEN

Of course, my treacherous tears arrived as soon as the heavy door closed behind me.

I made my way across the village square. It had once been a lively gathering place, but the Great September Fire had altered it permanently.

A stone fountain fed by a nearby stream had survived the fire. It featured a humming-bear, spitting water into the air, the base black from its brush with the inferno. From time to time, green doves and spotted Tenner's squirrels sipped at the fountain.

The old carousel nearby sat motionless. For the most part, it had escaped the fire's wrath. I sat next to the sole blue willow in the square that had come through the fire unscathed. Leaning against its smooth-barked trunk, I removed Connor's puzzler from my pocket.

The twirling tusks. The strange tail. The homely snout.

I began to cry. I cried for my ma and pa and little brother, for Sir Zurt, for Duuzuu with his singed wings, for everyone everywhere. I cried for myself because I was alone and lonely on my birthday. And because I was odd and unlovable.

For a long time, I let myself weep.

Angry tears, indeed.

They held no magic. Just despair.

After a while, I felt calmer. I wiped my poor,

damp puzzler. Bits of mud and stone had fallen off, and one of its ears had chipped.

I should have been more careful. Even my tears were clumsy.

The meeting finally ended, and I watched the villagers streaming out of the hall. I wondered if they'd come to any decisions. What plans could they really make? To hope with more fury? To bicker with more energy?

They were the grown-ups. They were in charge. And yet I'd seen children behave better.

I wondered if Connor would notice me. I wasn't too far from the door. I wondered, too, if I had embarrassed him with my outburst. No doubt.

A few minutes later, Connor exited with his father and two other men, all deep in conversation. Connor's eyes fell on me.

I imagined how I must look. Tear-streaked face, mouth locked in a frown, all alone with my screecher.

Connor sent me a smile. Mr. Burke nudged him along, as if I had the red fever. As if my mere existence posed some kind of threat.

It was unusually warm. The afternoon sun was putting on a persuasive show. I stood and slipped the screecher back into my pocket. Then I took off my coat and set it on the carousel's blue wooden unicorn.

In front of the unicorn stood a gold spotted pony. He'd lost his tail and a front hoof in the fire. He wasn't anyone's favorite, so of course he was mine. I climbed on and pretended I could ride where no one else could find me. Where I was alone with the world I loved, the world as I remembered it. The world I couldn't bring back.

I sat there for a long time, letting the sun soak in, waiting in vain for it to warm my heart. After a while, I gave up and headed home.

I was almost back to the cottage when

I remembered that I'd left my coat behind, with the screecher tucked inside the pocket.

When I returned to the carousel, my coat was still there.

And so was the screecher.

Unharmed. Untouched.

And very much alive.

Part Three

The screecher sits near the base of the blue willow.
She senses movement.

Someone is coming!

Her head turns. She sees something. An animal
with long, red head fur and four appendages.

The red-furred animal takes a step forward.

Her scent is familiar. But how could that
possibly be?

And is she safe?

Thwap.

The attachment on the screecher's rear end

strikes the ground. She is not sure why. It seems to have a mind of its own.

A pungent aroma fills the air. It is full of worry and warning.

But the red-furred animal is still coming. She moves awkwardly, but there is something gentle about her, too.

What to do? Run? Hide? Stay perfectly still?

Is this what it's like to be alive?

Will the screecher ever know everything she needs to know? Will she always be torn between hope and fear?

Why is this happening? What curious magic has brought her to this moment?

CHAPTER
TWENTY

I didn't dare move.

I couldn't bear to frighten the trembling animal away.

The familiar scent of scared screecher wafted my way.

I glanced right and left. The square was deserted, save for a lirkmunk who chittered in annoyance at the smell and ran for the safety of a nearby thicket.

Behind me, down toward the river, villagers

were setting up stalls to sell their wares for the Faire, ever hopeful.

Before me sat a baby screecher. My coat was lying on the ground nearby. Even from here, I could see that the pocket was empty.

I had always been a practical sort. I did not believe in magic, in spells, in things that defied logic. As it was, nature provided plenty of mystery.

I inched closer. The baby screecher's eyes were huge with fear.

It was roughly the same size as the puzzler Connor had given me.

It was in roughly the same place that I'd left the puzzler.

And the puzzler seemed to be gone.

But.

But it was a huge leap, a giant chasm of a leap, to think that one thing had turned into the other.

That was not how nature worked. Baby screechers didn't just suddenly appear out of thin air.

It was a female, I decided, based on her small snout and narrow chest. Clearly she had wandered here from the woods.

It was a bizarre coincidence. That's all it was.

The screecher made a squeaky noise. A warning to me, perhaps? It was all I could do not to laugh.

I'd seen baby screechers before, that time with my pa. And a couple years back, I'd even caught a glimpse of a ma screecher with four newborns. (I'd backed away lightning quick. I knew the last thing the ma needed right then was a human intruder.)

Even when they were young, I had to admit that screechers were odd-looking animals, and this one was no exception. Still, when she tried to take a step and tumbled onto her tail, it was awfully charming. Her tusks weren't much to look at, and her tail bristles seemed more delicate than threatening. But I knew she was meant to grow into something fearsome.

Where could she have come from? There weren't any nests nearby. I would have seen them. Or Connor would have.

Perhaps a hunter had killed its ma? Maybe the baby had wandered down from the hills, somehow surviving.

It was incredibly unlikely. But there had to be an explanation.

Poor thing.

I took another step, and she gave what was supposed to be a fierce growl, like a crabby kitten, then whacked her tail again.

It didn't have much effect. The air smelled as bad as it was going to get, given her size.

I couldn't leave her here. She'd be dead by

nightfall. I thought of Otwel Borwan and shuddered.

I knelt down, looked away, and backed up to show I wasn't a threat. The screecher seemed to calm a bit.

Slowly I kept moving away. The baby busied herself licking her tail. I circled around until I was on the far side of the carousel, mostly hidden by the legs of the wooden animals.

The screecher's ears pricked up. One of them had a notch in it, just like Connor's puzzler.

I couldn't think about that now.

She had a reed bow tied around her neck, just like Connor's puzzler.

But I couldn't think about that, either.

The baby could hear me moving as I reached up to pull my coat off the blue unicorn. But she seemed to be distracted by the desire to make her four legs work together.

I would only have one chance.

Deep breath. I took a flying leap off the carousel, stretched out my arms, and trapped the baby screecher under my coat.

If she'd been any bigger, her shrieks of outrage would have been deafening.

TWENTY-ONE

While she struggled and squeaked, I wrapped her up as best I could. I reminded myself that even though she was young, her tail quills might hurt me. I'd heard the quills of adult screechers caused a miserable sting and took forever to remove.

I held her close to my chest. "Shh," I said. "Hush, little one. You'll be all right."

I didn't want to squeeze too hard, didn't want to crush the terrified baby or prevent her from getting enough air. But I also wanted to keep her quiet enough for me to sneak through the village center and make my way back to Mae and Birdie's cottage.

I could try to cut through the woods, but around here, they were thick with briar bushes. I'd have a hard time getting through, even without having to hold a squirmy baby.

On the other hand, once again I bore screecher perfume, which would make it difficult for me to pass unnoticed.

"Shh, now," I whispered. "We're going to find a safe place for you." Even as I said the words, I realized I had no idea where that would be.

What would I feed the baby? Would it need mother's milk? What if there was a nest hidden away somewhere with more babies? Or an injured adult?

Nothing I could do about it now.

Something scratched my arm, and I realized it was the screecher's claws. They'd pierced right through my coat. Not much of a mark, but still. It made me realize how powerful adult claws must be.

I began to walk, humming softly, and maybe it was the rhythmic movement, or my off-key tune, but the baby seemed to relax. I stayed away from the riverfront, where most of the activity was, and kept to a back path. But I passed several villagers, a few of whom I recognized from the council meeting.

"Look," an old man said, "it's the screecher girl."

"She certainly smells the part," said his companion.

I kept my gaze straight ahead, clutched my coat, and moved as fast as I could, ignoring the occasional taunts or eye rolls.

As I approached the lane leading to the cottage, I glanced down at the riverfront. The blue willows spiraled in the brisk, warm wind. I saw no hummingbears.

I did, however, see Connor. He was hammering a wooden stall into place. A stack of his hummingbear puzzlers sat nearby in a large willow basket. Quickly I averted my gaze, but not before he noticed me.

"Willodeen!" he yelled. "Wait!"

"I'm in a hurry," I called over my shoulder. He grabbed the basket and ran to catch up with me, even as I increased my pace.

"Wait!" he repeated. "I want to explain!"

A moment later, Connor had joined me, moving in tandem with my stride. He was breathless, his face anxious.

"I should have spoken up at the meeting," he said. "Defended you."

"Why?" I asked. "It's not like it would have mattered."

"Because I agreed with you. But my father is . . . I knew he'd be embarrassed if I—" Connor paused, sniffing the air. "I could swear I smell screecher."

"Hmm," I said, holding my coat tighter. I wanted to show him what I'd found. But my confusion about the screecher's origins made me wary. Could I trust Connor? Would he tell his father?

Already I felt strangely protective about the baby. The way, I supposed, a parent must feel about a child.

The road narrowed and grew steeper, and our pace slowed a bit. The baby let out a noise that sounded like a squirrel's squeak. It was hard to ignore.

Connor frowned. "What was that?"

"Just me." I coughed loudly. "Might be catching. You'd best be on your way."

"But—"

I stopped. "Connor, it's all fine, really. There was no point in you speaking up at the council meeting, because there was no point in *my* speaking up. Nobody cares about screechers. It's the hummingbears they're worried about, and I understand that, I do, but—*ouch!*"

The baby had poked its claws into my neck.

I loosened my grip just a tad, and out popped her little screecher head, comical tusks and all.

Apparently, she'd had quite enough of my company. She wriggled free, dropped to the ground with a squeal, and took off running.

It seemed she'd figured out how to use those feet, after all.

TWENTY-TWO

The baby scrambled up the road with surprising speed.

"It's a screecher!" Connor said.

"We have to catch it," I yelled, already running. "Or they will!"

I didn't have to tell Connor who "they" were.

The screecher still hadn't quite grasped the art of running. Her legs got tangled quickly. She dashed, tripped, landed on her rear or sometimes her snout, then dashed off some more. Back and forth across the road she darted in a random zigzag.

Other than a cottage or two, thick woods edged up against both sides of the road. I kept waiting for the baby to disappear into the underbrush. Instinct would urge her there, I thought. But she seemed too overwhelmed to know what to do, which was a good thing for us.

Connor dumped out his basket of humming-bear puzzlers, then bounded ahead. In a flash, he was on the far side of the baby, planted solidly in the middle of the road with his empty basket at the ready.

The screecher caught sight of him. She paused, glanced behind her, and there I was, my coat held open.

"She'll head into the trees!" I called. "Try not to scare her."

Connor's look said I was stating the obvious.

The screecher squeaked, circled, reared up

on her hind legs, and toppled onto her side. Poor thing. She was so confused, so lost.

I met Connor's eyes. He nodded.

I held up one finger, then two, and on three we ran for her. She bolted, heading to my right toward a tangle of sunberry bushes. But Connor and I were faster.

Connor dropped his basket over her. Carefully we slid my coat under the overturned basket, then upended it.

Once again, she was trapped.

Connor and I looked at each other. Breathless, dirty, sprawled in the road. "Good work," I said, brushing my hair out of my eyes.

"Where did you find it?" Connor asked.

"Down by the carousel. I left my coat behind, and when I went back, she was just sitting there."

Connor peeked under my coat. The baby attempted a winsome snarl.

"Willodeen," he said. "Its neck."

I rubbed the spot where the baby had poked me. "It's nothing. I'll get it cleaned back at the cottage."

"Not your neck. *Its* neck." He seemed frustrated. "Did you see what's around its neck?"

I didn't answer.

"A sweetgrass reed."

I waited for more.

"A sweetgrass reed. Tied in a bow."

I looked at my shoes.

"The screecher I gave you had a sweetgrass reed tied in a bow around its neck."

I swallowed. The baby screecher skittered back and forth in the basket.

"Did you put that bow on the baby?"

"No," I said. "Maybe it got tangled in some reeds. Or maybe someone did it as a prank. Or . . ." I was out of ideas.

"I suppose." Connor patted the pockets of my coat. "Where's the puzzler I gave you?" he asked.

"I'm, uh, not exactly sure."

Connor frowned. "You mean it's gone?"

"I . . ." I hoped that if I said the words quickly enough, they wouldn't sound so absurd. "I accidentally left my coat on the carousel—you know the blue unicorn?—well, that's where I left it, and then I went back to get it and the puzzler was gone and there was this baby on the ground with a bow and my pocket was empty and really that's all I know."

Connor stared at the basket. Then he stared at me.

I didn't say the other thing I knew. That the baby screecher had a notched ear. That my own tears had made a similar nick in Connor's puzzler.

I didn't say it because I couldn't let myself believe there was any connection.

"We should go back," I said, pointing down the hill. "All your hummingbear puzzlers are there."

"That's the least of our problems," Connor said with a weary smile.

The baby squeaked. She did not sound happy.

"Let's go see Mae and Birdie," I suggested. "They'll know what to do."

I wondered if Connor could hear the doubt in my voice.

TWENTY-THREE

Mae and Birdie did not seem particularly surprised to find a basket containing a baby screecher arriving at their door. Strangely enough, the baby screecher didn't seem particularly surprised, either.

We placed the basket before the hearth. It was warm in the cottage, but Birdie lit a fire, anyway. Even after I slid my coat off the top of the basket, the baby sat calmly, peering up at us with her vigilant green eyes, rimmed in yellow. Perhaps she had used all her energy trying to run away. Or maybe she found the crackling fire calming.

Duuzuu seemed fascinated by our new addition. He hopped over to Connor, fluttered up to his shoulder, and gazed down at the baby, cooing questions.

Gently as I could, I slipped the sweetgrass reed over the screecher's head. She grumbled unconvincingly.

I passed the bow to Connor. He examined it, slowly shaking his head.

"Poor wee thing," said Mae. "Must be scared to death."

Birdie set a saucer of water in front of the baby. The screecher lapped it up eagerly.

"So is there a reason we have this visitor?" Birdie asked as she refilled the saucer.

I hesitated, but only for a second. I knew we were going to share the whole story with

Mae and Birdie. They were probably the only people in the world we *could* tell without being laughed at or locked away. And at least the baby would be safe here.

I recounted what had happened, with some help from Connor. The screecher's appearance on the carousel, my empty coat pocket, the attempted escape, the reed tied around its neck.

Connor held up the bow. "It has to be the same one," he murmured. He looked from Mae to Birdie and back again. "Doesn't it?"

Mae settled in a rocker near the basket. "What were you doing before he appeared, Willodeen?" She squinted at the baby. "Or is he a she?"

"A she, I'm pretty sure," I said.

"She'll be needing a name, then," Birdie pointed out.

Mae held up her hand. "First things first,

Bird. What was happening before you found her, Willodeen?"

"I went to the council meeting with Connor."

"She spoke up, too," said Connor. I was surprised to hear something in his voice that sounded like pride.

Birdie clapped her hands together. "Brava!" she cried. "Did you unburden yourself? Make your case?"

"Oh, I unburdened, all right." I really didn't want to go into the details. "And then I went outside. And I sat down and I . . ."

"Did you cry?" Mae asked. She actually looked hopeful.

"I guess so. I mean, yes. I was mad."

"Aha! Angry tears!" Mae declared with a triumphant smile. She nodded at Birdie. "That's got to be it."

"Without a doubt," Birdie agreed.

"Angry tears have magic in them," Mae

explained to Connor, but he didn't appear to need convincing.

"That would explain it," he said, cradling Duuzuu in the crook of his arm.

I shot him a glance to see if he was making fun. But no, Connor seemed to be in complete agreement.

"You can't be serious," I said, rubbing my eyes. "All three of you actually believe this?"

Mae put her hand near her mouth and said, in a stage whisper, "Willodeen doesn't believe in magic."

Connor looked disappointed. "Really? Is that true?"

"Of course it's true," I said. "You do?"

"I believe there are things we don't understand," he said.

"That doesn't mean magic exists," I replied.

"There's magic in all of us," Birdie said. "Just a bit. You're born with it, like fingers and toes and fuzzy baby hair. Some of us make use of it. And some do not."

We sat in silence for a few minutes, the only sounds coming from the shifting logs in the fire and Duuzuu's occasional questioning coos.

Birdie gave the baby more water. "I wonder how she got that notch in her right ear?" she mused.

I cleared my throat.

I looked at Connor and Birdie and Mae, all three of them ready, apparently, to believe anything about the creature in our midst.

I sighed.

Then I told them about my tears. And about the nick they'd made in Connor's puzzler.

We all gazed down at the baby, as if her ear held the answer to the world's most pressing questions.

"I believe," Mae said at last, "that you have just proved our point, Willodeen, dear."

Before I could respond, the baby let loose a pitiful cry.

"We can debate this another day," said Birdie. "Magic or not, right now, we've got ourselves a hungry baby screecher, and nothing at all to feed it."

CHAPTER

TWENTY-FOUR

I consulted my notebooks and tried to remember everything Pa had ever told me about screechers. Then I made a list of any food I thought they might eat, while Birdie cleaned the scratch on my neck with a cloth soaked in one of her horrible-smelling salves.

It wasn't a very appetizing list. Worms. Grubs. Dilly bugs. Slugs. Peacock snails. Pink mushrooms. Aspen twigs. Sunferns.

I didn't know where to start.

"She's so young," I said. "I suppose she might still need mother's milk."

Birdie sighed. "I've not a clue."

"Nor I," said Mae.

"I've seen screechers rooting near blue willows and berry bushes," Connor offered. "Come to think of it, I've even seen them digging through trash bins in the village."

"Some animals will only eat a few things," I said. "Hummingbears are known for being picky. They like aphids, flies, and blue willow leaves, and that's about it."

"The one in our home is definitely the exception to that rule," said Mae, leveling a finger at Duuzuu. "I'm talking to you, cake stealer."

"I just don't know where to start," I said.

"You probably know more about screechers than the rest of the village put together, Willodeen," Connor said.

I reached out my right index finger toward

the baby, hoping to scratch the top of her head. She looked so hopeful, and so helpless.

The baby promptly bit my finger. "Ouch!" I cried. She didn't break my skin, but I was going to have to be careful of her sharp baby teeth and those twisting tusks.

She looked quite proud of herself. And not nearly so helpless.

"'And though she be but little, she is fierce,'" said Mae. "Shakespeare. *A Midsummer Night's Dream*."

Birdie sighed. "Remember the production in Somerset? What a superb Titania you were!"

"Bird, you are too kind." Mae waved a hand. "But we digress. What might we feed our new arrival?"

"You've both come up with recipes before," I said. "Remember the baby hedgehog we found? And that abandoned tiger fox pup?

Maybe you could come up with something for a screecher."

"It couldn't hurt to try," said Mae.

Connor shifted uncomfortably. "I really should go. My father will be wondering where I am."

"Will he be mad?" I asked.

"He doesn't get mad." Connor smiled. "He gets disappointed."

"Don't you worry, Connor," said Mae. "We'll take good care of the wee one."

"Your puzzlers!" I exclaimed. "You'll need your basket."

"Puzzlers?" Birdie repeated.

"We left Connor's hummingbear sculptures on the side of the road. We needed his basket to capture the baby."

"You can use that wooden crate in the kitchen for a bed," said Birdie. "The one with potatoes and turnips in it."

I emptied the crate, and Mae gave me an old quilt to line it. Connor and I tilted his basket over the crate, and the baby slid out like a sledder on a snowy hill. To my surprise, she didn't seem at all annoyed.

"I think she actually enjoyed that," Connor said, laughing.

Birdie tapped her finger on her chin. "You know, she does need a name."

I looked at Connor. My mind was a blank.

He thought for a moment. "She seems like a Quinby to me."

"Quinby?" I said.

"I had a dog named Quinby once. Used to howl at night like a coyote. Or a screecher."

I leaned toward the basket. "Quinby?" I whispered.

She responded with a squeaky noise. I can't say that it was a pleasant noise. But I took it to be a good sign.

"All right, Duuzuu," I said. "Say goodbye to Connor."

"Off you go, Duuzuu," Connor said, nudging him over to my shoulder.

"Good luck with your father," I said.

"Good luck with your screecher," he said.

I knew we would need it. Luck, skill, maybe even a bit of magic.

CHAPTER
TWENTY-FIVE

The next two days were a blur of mixing, cutting, hunting, and a whole lot of guessing as we tried to coax Quinby to eat.

Our first concoction included one mealworm, a piece of fern, two sunberries, and pinches of salt and sugar. Mae and Birdie mashed it all up with a mortar and pestle and added a bit of warm water, and then it was my turn.

I dipped a scrap of fabric into the awful-looking mess, then squeezed out droplets, aiming for Quinby's mouth. Pa and I had done something similar with an abandoned baby wistbird we'd nursed back to health. That nestling had opened his beak so wide he could have swallowed the very egg he'd pecked his way out of.

He had been easy to feed.

Quinby, unfortunately, was not.

She let the mixture drip onto her snout. Then she shook her head and grumbled at me.

"Could be she's ready for solid food," I said. "Some critters wean quickly."

Next we tried all manner of bugs and vegetation. We cut everything into pieces, set a plate in front of Quinby, and stepped back, watching and hoping.

Quinby sniffed once, twice, then backed away, as if we'd deeply offended her.

"She's shivering," I said as I removed the plate.

We'd already tried to cover her with Mae's

quilt, but Quinby had shaken it off. Mae provided another one of her shawls, and I created a cozy nest for Quinby. That, at least, she seemed to appreciate.

"I'm worried," I told Birdie and Mae as we sipped hot peppermint tea at the kitchen table. "What if she won't eat? What if she just wastes away?"

"If anyone knows screechers, it's you," Birdie said. "You'll figure it out."

"I don't know anything about *magic* screechers," I said.

"Expect they eat same as the regular ones," said Mae.

I sat at the kitchen table, poring over my notebooks. Looking for hints about screecher behavior I might have missed. Each entry brought back a memory, the way a familiar smell can instantly transport you to another place and time.

Three and a half years ago, I'd watched two

screechers eat a purple toadlet. Peacock snails came up frequently in my notes, year after year, but they were difficult to find these days. The autumn before last, I'd seen two adult screechers eating spotted oak moths.

Well, there was nothing to do but keep trying. I heaved a sigh. Since we'd captured Quinby, I hadn't seen Connor. I hoped he hadn't gotten into any trouble with his father about the puzzlers. Or about spending time with me.

Truth was, it would have been useful to have Connor help me forage for Quinby's food. Not that I wanted his company, exactly. But an extra pair of hands digging for worms wouldn't have been the worst thing in the world.

"I'm going out to look again," I announced.

"We'll keep an eye on Quinby," said Mae. "Good hunting."

"It's heading toward twilight," said Birdie. "Best take a lantern."

"I'll be back before dark, Birdie."

Birdie clucked her tongue. "Stubborn as the day is long," she said, and we both smiled. How many times, since I'd moved in, had she uttered those same words to me?

Still, remembering how I'd needed to borrow Connor's lantern, I relented and grabbed one.

Duuzuu noticed me donning my coat and made his questioning noise. Normally, he would have fluttered over to my shoulder, anxious to go outside. But since Quinby's arrival, he'd spent all his time perched on a chair near her crate, like a worried big brother.

"Good luck," Mae called, and Duuzuu sent me a soft, encouraging coo.

It was another strange day of autumn weather. The Dragon Sighs were strong, whipping past in sudden bursts, and it was so warm I considered removing my coat. I kicked through piles of crisp, brown leaves and savored the sound. All the while, I kept my eyes open for bugs or greens that might appeal to our hungry baby screecher.

I headed up the road. Connor had mentioned a small stand of blue willows up that way, and I thought I might find something there. Like him, I'd seen screechers digging near blue willow roots now and then. There were two other spots where I'd found screechers nesting in the past, and I planned to check those areas, too. I removed my notebook from my waistpouch to make certain I remembered the precise locations.

As I thumbed through the pages, I heard someone call my name.

It was Connor. And he was with his father.

My first instinct was to duck into the

bushes. I wasn't exactly sure why. But after my performance at the council meeting, I had a feeling Mr. Burke might best be avoided.

"Willodeen!" Connor yelled. "Up here!"

Apparently, hiding was not an option. I took a deep breath, and up the hill I went.

TWENTY-SIX

"Father, this is Willodeen," Connor said as I neared.

"Ah, yes. From the council meeting," said Mr. Burke. I expected a mocking tone, but didn't hear one, so I made myself meet his eyes.

To my surprise, his gaze was thoughtful, maybe even kind. Somehow, close up, he looked tired and weathered, less intimidating than he had at the meeting. I could see Connor in him, and him in Connor.

Connor rubbed the back of his neck. "How is . . . everything?"

"Fine," I answered, and I was relieved we both seemed to understand there would be no talk of Quinby in front of his father. I pointed to the paper Connor was holding. "What's that?"

"A map," he said. "They're thinking about expanding the rail route. Father and I came up to get a better look at things."

Below us, village lights glowed in the shadow of the hills as twilight descended. From this height, Perchance seemed puny and fragile, as delicate as one of Connor's puzzlers.

"They're proposing a cut through Sutton's Ridge." Mr. Burke pointed northeast. "It would bring the railroad closer to the river and the mill."

We were buffeted by a fresh gust of wind. The trees shivered, our coats ballooned, and the map nearly flew out of Connor's hands.

"Dragon Sighs are fierce this year," Connor said, struggling to fold the map.

"Last time they were like this was, what, two years back?" Mr. Burke asked. "That's when we had the Roundtop Ridge Fire, the one that started up near the tracks."

As if on cue, a steam engine chugged through the hills just west of us. We could see its dark, confident body, its steamy breath. As it braked to a slow halt, red sparks sprayed.

"At the meeting," I said, and then I paused, suddenly self-conscious. "Um, that man—Mr. Williams, I think—said something about the railroad and the fires."

"They've cleared brush near the tracks, best as they can, I'm told," said Mr. Burke. "Only so much we can do, though. The railroad doesn't much care what we have to say, and they own the land."

Connor pointed to a cleared strip of forest where a stand of blue willows had been planted a year ago. "Those willows don't look like they're doing well," he said.

"I told them it was a bad idea to plant there. Blue willows crave water. Ponds, rivers, lakes." Mr. Burke shook his head. "But we were outnumbered. The train brings tourists. The blue willows bring humming-bears. Everybody should be happy. Only it doesn't always work out that way." He gave a short laugh. "That's what they like to call progress."

Another blast of hot wind came, so strong I almost lost my balance. I dropped my note-book, and Mr. Burke knelt down and handed it to me.

"Are you an artist like Connor?" he asked.

"No," I said, quickly returning the note-book to my waistpouch. "I . . . I take notes on things. The woods. The animals. Changes."

I wondered if he'd scoff, but he merely nod-ded. "A scholar, then."

I didn't have the nerve to tell him I rarely attended school. A scholar I definitely was not.

"Well, good for you. The world is changing. We're going to need scientists, inventors, people who look at everything in fresh ways. I visited the capital last month. Whole town lit by gas lamps. It was a wonder to see. Perchance has some catching up to do."

"We'll always need artists, too," I said, smiling at Connor. He looked at his feet, the way I so often did.

"Perhaps," said Mr. Burke, brow creased. "I just worry about . . . the future. It's my job as a parent."

We fell silent, gazing at the village as the sun shot crimson arrows through the trees.

"You know," Mr. Burke mused after a spell, "Connor's mother used to do that. Keep a notebook."

I wasn't sure what to say. Connor had never mentioned his mother before.

"For her it was birds," Mr. Burke continued. "She drew them, studied them, counted them. That's probably where Connor got his artistic abilities."

"Does she still keep a notebook?" I asked.

"She died of the red fever when Connor was three."

"Oh. I . . . I didn't know."

What did you say to people who'd lost someone they loved? What did people say to me?

Nothing that ever changed anything.

"I'm sorry," I said, too softly and too late.

"Well, we should get going," said Mr. Burke. "Good to meet you, Willodeen."

I nodded to them both and started off. But a moment later, I heard Connor running after me. "Is Quinby all right?" he whispered.

"She's not eating," I said. "That's why I'm out here. Thought I might find some peacock snails or red leaf beetles. I'm running out of ideas."

"I'll come by tomorrow to help. I couldn't today or yesterday. I had to repair a lot of those puzzlers."

"I'm sorry about that."

He grinned. "It was worth it," he said. He pointed toward a cluster of fir trees.

"If you're looking for peacock snails, there's that grove of blue willows I told you about. Just five of them, hidden away, but it might be worth a try. Go that way"—he pointed to my left—"and listen for a stream."

"I'll check it out."

Connor crossed his fingers. I watched him lope down the hill to catch up with his father. As I headed into the trees, the high-pitched whistle of a steam engine carried on the wind, harsh and plaintive as a screecher's call.

CHAPTER

TWENTY-SEVEN

That evening, I tried feeding Quinby some petals from a late-blooming silver pansy.

She practically sneered.

I gave her the pulverized wing of a spotted oak moth.

No luck.

I presented her with the two red leaf beetles I'd managed to find under a decaying log.

Nope.

Finally, I placed a saucer of peacock snails in front of her.

Quinby let out a screech of joy. She planted her two front feet in the saucer and gobbled down those snails so quickly I was afraid she'd choke.

Duuzuu watched from his perch near Quinby's crate, cooing nervously at her table manners.

"Well, well," said Birdie. "I think you've found the magic recipe, Willodeen."

The snails were the size of my thumbnail, and their swirling, multicolored shells were soft to the touch. I'd managed to find five of them by digging, with great effort, at the base of the blue willows Connor had told me about.

It hadn't been easy. The snails liked to burrow deep beneath the tangled tree roots. My knuckles were bloodied, my fingernails black with soil.

I sighed with satisfaction. It felt so good to have provided for Quinby.

A memory came to me. My pa, watching the screecher and her babies, saying: *She's just doing what she's meant to do, my girl. Caring for her own, best as she can. Like all us mas and pas.*

Still, I felt for the poor peacock snails. After all, they were living creatures, too. But that was the way of things, wasn't it? Didn't I eat hens' eggs and river trout and venison?

"I feel guilty about the snails," I admitted. "They're so pretty. And there they were, minding their own business, until I came along."

Birdie, who was chopping onions, nodded. "Nature's complicated that way. I know some folks who will only eat things that grow in

160

the ground." She thought for a moment. "Not sure where peacock snails would fit into that equation."

Quinby's belly expanded like a coin purse filling with gold. "The snails were so hard to get to," I said.

"You could try the blue willows down by the riverfront," said Mae as her knitting needles clicked away.

"And there's that new grove," said Birdie. "Although those trees are still pretty young."

"Connor's father said those trees need more water," I said.

"You saw his father?" asked Mae.

"And Connor," I said. "At the top of the ridge. There's talk of the railroad expanding."

"Ahh," said Mae.

"Is that a good 'ahh,'" I asked, "or a bad one?"

"Neither," said Mae. "Change is coming, certain as sunrise. The only question is how we deal with it."

I sat back, arms behind my head, watching Quinby lick her dish clean. "What am I going to do with her? She can't stay here forever. She's a wild thing. Unless, of course . . ."

"Unless?" said Birdie.

"I don't know. Unless she isn't . . . real. Unless this magic is going to pass."

"Looks pretty real to me," said Birdie.

Mae laughed. "Certainly eats like she's real."

I basked in their good-hearted smiles, as warming as the fire. Taking me in must have completely upended their lives. The same way taking in Quinby was complicating my life.

"Thank you," I murmured.

"For what?" Birdie asked.

"For letting me be here," I said. "And Duu-zuu. And Quinby."

"Fiddle-faddle," said Birdie.

"I second her fiddle-faddle," said Mae.

That night I settled into bed with Duuzuu and Quinby beside me.

They both snored. It was like they were having a conversation.

I smiled. I wished Connor could hear them.

Closing my eyes, I wondered if sleep would play hide-and-seek with me tonight, as it so often did.

I needn't have worried. The gentle snores of my two companions made for a perfect lullaby.

Part Four

The screecher awakens in her nest—is that what it
is?—and listens to the night world.

The nest has hard, flat sides that smell of trees,
and an open top. She is wrapped in warmth that
makes her heart slow, her breathing calm.

How full she is! How good it is to finally eat
what her body seems to know it needs!

She has seen two kinds of animals thus far in
her short life.

One is fur-covered and winged. He perches
close, watching her with wide eyes. He is different

in many ways. But he is more like her than the other animals she has met.

They are tall and clumsy in their movements, always making strange noises, sweet highs and gruff lows and long exhalations. Whatever they are, they haven't hurt her.

The first time they'd reached into her nest, she'd recoiled.

Wetness was there. Water.

She'd had no idea how thirsty she was.

More?

More came.

More?

And more.

Then food.

Green, brown, wet, alive, dead. All wrong.

She'd waited.

Patience had served her well so far.

And then, there it was. The right food, at last.

If she keeps eating, she may survive. If she

survives, she may learn how to be whatever she is meant to be.

Being alive takes all the energy she can muster. But it seems to be full of possibilities.

She will take her time. She will hope. She will rely on others, on these strange animals who study her so carefully.

She has no other choice.

Nearby, the red-furred animal, the food-bringer, is sleeping. On her pillow is the small flying beast. He opens one eye and lets out a soft trill.

The screecher returns his gaze. She replies with a sound that's new to her, a grumbly purr.

The flying beast goes back to sleep.

Moonlight pours in and pools in the nest. Night is when another kind of sound happens, but she's not ready for that. Not yet.

TWENTY-EIGHT

Connor and I spent the next morning trying to unearth more peacock snails. He brought the knife he used for cutting reeds, and I borrowed a trowel from Mae and Birdie's garden. After two hours, three cuts, several scraped knuckles, and endless holes, we had only eight snails to show for our efforts.

"It looks so easy when the screechers do it," I said, stretching my weary arms. "No matter where we dig, it ends up being the wrong place."

"Wait a minute!" Connor exclaimed. His smile got lopsided when he was excited. "Maybe that's the answer. What if we let Quinby do the digging?"

The very thought made me panic. "But what if she runs off? What if a hunter sees her?"

"I have an idea," Connor said. "Give me an hour."

By noon, we were back at the cottage, with the strange contraption Connor had created out of reeds and willow branches. As soon as we entered, Duuzuu fluttered over to Connor's shoulder, and Quinby poked her head over the side of her crate, her snout quivering.

"Well, what have we here?" Mae asked, looking up from her never-ending knitting.

"It's a harness," I said. "For Quinby. At least we hope it is."

I placed Quinby's peacock snails on a plate, and she ate them in a flash. She sent me a hopeful look. "Sorry, girl," I said. "That's all we could find."

"We're going to let Quinby do her own hunting," Connor explained.

"I like your thinking," said Mae.

First we had to get Quinby into the harness, and that was a tall order. Her claws were already longer and sharper.

Gingerly, I picked her up by the scruff of her neck, the way a mother dog would hold a puppy. With Connor, Mae, and Birdie all working at once, we managed to slip the harness over Quinby's head and ease her two front paws through the holes.

I found some rope, and Connor tied it to two loops he'd made on top of the harness.

"If that isn't a ridiculous sight," said Birdie. "But an ingenious one."

We let Quinby roam the cottage so she could get used to the harness. She moved around like a tin soldier, her legs stiff, trying in vain to grab the rope with her teeth. She was clearly not happy with us.

"I really don't want to do this," I said. "It doesn't feel right, having a wild thing tied up. But if she were to run away, I don't know what I'd do." I frowned. "We're hoping she'll be able to scent out peacock snails better than we can."

"Not to mention dig them," Connor added.

Connor had brought his basket, and we loaded Quinby in that, along with Mae's blanket. The basket had two handles, so we each took a side, and Connor held the rope as well. I put my coat over the top, and off we went.

We passed a couple people on the road, but

nobody said a word, and Quinby, thankfully, was fairly quiet, although she poked her nose out a couple times to take in the exciting new smells.

By the time we reached the hidden grove where we'd dug that morning, Quinby was making eager squeaking noises and scratching at the sides of the basket.

"I wonder what she's thinking," Connor said.

"Me too," I said. "Probably trying to figure out what the ridiculous humans are up to."

We slid her out of the basket. Quinby blinked, stunned. She looked up and down and all around. She pulled on her rope to get close to the willow roots.

And then she went to work.

If you've ever seen a dog bury a bone, or a spotted green chipmunk rooting for a lost acorn, you will know what I'm talking about. Quinby clawed near those trees with utter

certainty she'd reach her goal. Every so often, she'd stop to sniff the ground, her snout quivering. And every time she dug, she found a treasure trove of peacock snails. Dozens upon dozens.

"She knows exactly where to dig," I said. "Their sense of smell is amazing."

"And their actual smell," Connor joked. "When screechers were invented, Mother Nature made them scented."

I laughed. "I've never heard that before. My pa would've liked it."

It was strange, hearing myself say "pa" out loud. I couldn't remember the last time I had.

"I made it up just now." Connor tightened his grip on Quinby's rope. "I've actually been trying to write a story about Quinby. About how she must feel. And how she came to be." He gave an embarrassed smile. "It's not very good."

"I doubt that." I hesitated. "Maybe . . . maybe I could read it someday."

"I still don't know how it ends. I don't even know much about her yet."

"That's what I like about watching screechers. Trying to figure all that out. Like your ma with the birds, I s'pose."

I cast a sidelong glance to see if I'd made a mistake bringing up Connor's ma. But he was smiling, same as me.

"She would have liked you, I think," Connor said. "My mother."

"I bet I would've liked her, too."

He scratched his forehead, looking bemused. "You know, it's funny. I don't think I've talked to anyone about my mother in years. Except maybe my father. And hardly even then."

"I know what you mean." I stared at Quinby so Connor wouldn't see the tears forming in my eyes. "It's tough for most folks to understand. Unless . . . unless they've gone through it."

We didn't say anything more.

We didn't have to.

While Connor watched Quinby dig and eat, I pulled out my notebook and jotted down anything and everything. I walked around the five willows, trying to count the number of peacock snails Quinby ate. (She definitely seemed to prefer two trees in particular.) I felt the dirt, the twirling leaves. Using my feet, I measured the distance from the willows to the stream meandering downhill.

"What are you looking for?" Connor asked.

"I don't know," I admitted. "I never do. I just have the feeling that the looking will lead me to the right questions. And maybe even the right answers."

I worked on quietly. The only noises were the rustle of leaves, the scrabbling of Quinby's claws, and the stream talking. Silence filled with sound, it was.

We let Quinby eat until she looked over at us, her belly swollen, her eyes glazed, and gave a contented belch.

I wasn't certain how to tell if a screecher was happy, but I was pretty sure we carried one home that afternoon.

TWENTY-NINE

Every morning after that, Connor and I took Quinby back to the same spot. She quickly got used to the harness, which we removed as soon as she was safely back in the cottage. In fact, she seemed to associate it with snail hunting, and sat calmly as we slipped her into it.

Most days, Duuzuu joined us. He always rode on Connor's shoulder. Sometimes they talked to each other, one with words, one with coos, and I would just listen along.

Quinby was growing so fast that Connor decided to make a larger harness. We'd had to switch to a wheelbarrow, covered with a tarp, because she was too heavy to carry in the basket. Her tusks were sharper. Her tail quills were no longer soft to the touch. She drooled a bit, growled sometimes, and just generally looked less like a cute baby and more like the frightening animal she was meant to be. Still, Quinby never screeched at night. I often wondered why.

She'd also become more flexible about her diet. We'd gradually begun to add more foods, especially grubs and ferns, to her plates, and she would eat them when she ran out of peacock snails. But the snails were still clearly her favorite food.

One morning, Connor and I went uphill to find the Dragon Sighs kicking up whirlpools of dust. "Fire weather," Connor commented, and then he looked troubled. "Sorry," he said.

"No, it's all right." We never talked about the fire that had killed my family. But Connor knew what had happened.

"It must have been awful," he said.

"It was. But awful things happen to lots of people."

"True."

Our conversations were often like that, just a handful of words. I liked it. The silences were comfortable as an old sweater.

Walking in the forest with Connor was almost like walking alone. Like me, he was calm and watchful, although we were searching for different things. Connor was always on the lookout for petals and stones, reeds and cattails. I was always searching, unlikely as I knew it was, for more screechers. And of course, we both kept our eyes open for any hummingbears.

By the time we reached the hidden grove, Quinby was working hard to escape the wheelbarrow. As soon as we let her out, she dashed to a blue willow, nearly toppling me in her hurry.

Duuzuu, as always, sat on Connor's shoulder, preening himself. When he began cooing loudly and persistently, even Quinby turned to see what the commotion was about.

"I've decided Duuzuu makes three distinct noises," said Connor. "One for yes, one for no, and one for maybe."

"Which one is that?" I asked Connor.

"Oh, that's yes for sure," he said. "That's a very noisy yes."

"Calm down, Duuzuu," I chided, but his coos only grew more spirited. He craned his neck, and I followed his upward gaze.

There, settled into luminous bubble nests, were three hummingbears.

"Connor!" I whispered, pointing. "Look!"

He gasped. "I can't believe it! They're the first ones I've seen in ages." Duuzuu made a noise. "Well, except for you, of course."

"Poor Duuzuu," I said. "I wish he could join them. It's not fair."

"Lots of things aren't fair," Connor said, and I wondered if he was thinking about his ma, or maybe about my family.

We stared at the nests reflecting the sun, each one a little miracle. The hummingbears murmured to each other like doves.

"But why are they here?" I asked. "We haven't seen any by the riverfront. That's where they always used to migrate."

"There aren't any in those new groves they planted, either."

One of the hummingbears chewed a willow leaf. After a few minutes, he blew a glistening, perfectly round bubble, about the size of my palm. Carefully he added it to the top layer of his nest.

"It's amazing, the way the bubbles stick to each other," said Connor.

"And to the tree," I added. "But not to hummingbear fur. It must be something about the leaf sap."

"I wish I understood it. I'd love to make my puzzler pieces hold together like that."

"The bubbles are strong, too," I said. "I found one on the ground once and tried to pop it. I couldn't do it."

"Does Duuzuu ever make bubbles?"

"He used to," I said. "He doesn't bother much anymore. I guess my pillow is his nest now." I reached over to stroke Duuzuu's head. "I sure wish I knew why they've chosen this spot."

"Maybe because it's so secluded," Connor suggested. "Could be that hummingbears don't like crowds any more than you do."

I smiled. "But in years past, crowds didn't bother them. And they don't seem to mind that we're here. With a screecher, no less." I chewed on a thumbnail, considering. "We've brought Duuzuu a few times. I suppose his scent might have attracted them."

We waited until Quinby had eaten her fill of snails, then headed back to the cottage. Duuzuu, still on Connor's shoulder, chomped on a willow leaf as we walked. We were halfway down the hill, with Quinby dozing happily in the wheelbarrow, when I heard noises in the trees to my right.

I caught the glint of a rifle barrel. Three men crashed through the brush.

And one of them was Otwel Borwan, carrying his bow, with a quiver of arrows at the ready.

We froze.

"Well, if it ain't the screecher girl," said Otwel. He sauntered over, blocking our path forward. "What's in the barrow?"

I silently begged Quinby to stay still.

"Smells like something ripe," said his friend with the shotgun.

"Could be screecher," said the other.

I swallowed past a lump in my throat. About an inch of Quinby's tail was poking out from the tarp.

"Well, as you know, I always smell like screecher," I said as casually as I could.

Connor took a step forward. "Actually, it's manure," he said. "We've got plenty more than we need. Want some?"

"Dung and screechers." Otwel's lip curled. "Perfect company for ya, girl."

He backed up a couple paces, and we took that opportunity to swerve the barrow past the three men.

"You still owe me an arrow," Otwel called, but we were already rushing down the hill.

"That was close. Next time we might not be so lucky," Connor said as we neared the cottage. "We can't do this forever, Willodeen."

"I know," I said, panting. "I keep thinking we'll figure everything out."

We wheeled the barrow to the back of the cottage and let Quinby leap out. "My father's going to be thrilled to hear about the hummingbears," Connor said. "If more show up, maybe the Faire will actually happen, after all."

"Connor," I said. "Do you think maybe . . . could we wait just a day or two before we say anything about the hummingbears?"

"Why? Everyone will be so relieved."

"I know. I just feel like there's something I need to figure out. There are all these pieces, and if I can only look long enough . . . I know it doesn't make sense. I can't explain it."

"Sounds like my puzzlers," he said. "Sometimes you just have to give ideas room to breathe."

"One day?" I said.

He nodded. "Sure."

"Come on, Duuzuu," I said, holding out

my arm. Only then did I notice the little bubble he'd blown. It was oddly shaped, but he
clutched it in his paws, looking quite pleased.

When he let it go, we watched it float on
the air, impossibly strong, impossibly lovely.

CHAPTER
THIRTY

I woke that night to a horrible sound, a full-throated screaming into the blackness, screecher loud.

Only it wasn't a screecher.

It was me.

Mae and Birdie rushed into my room. Birdie held a flickering candle.

They perched on my bed, each taking a side. Duuzuu moved to my lap, and Quinby watched from the crate she'd nearly outgrown.

The wind toyed with my lace curtains. "Fire dream again?" asked Mae.

I nodded. In my head it was all still there.

The flames grabbing for me like a hungry monster.

The soles of my feet blistering.

The poisonous smoke scorching my lungs.

I looked at Birdie and Mae and asked the question. The one I'd asked a hundred times before. "Why?" I sobbed, then found my voice. "Why did I make it out when they didn't?"

They knew I meant my ma and pa and brother.

And I knew what they were going to say: what they always said.

No one knows why, Willodeen. But we are so glad you did.

I hated that answer.

I wanted adults to make sense of the world. I needed them to promise I would always be protected, even though I knew it was impossible. I yearned to hear "And they all lived happily ever after."

No one knows why. "Well, why not?" I wanted to scream.

And yet, despite all that, part of me welcomed their honesty. Birdie and Mae were grown-ups who weren't afraid to admit they didn't have all the answers.

It was scary. But it also sparked something inside me I couldn't explain. A feeling that maybe I could find the answers I needed, even if they couldn't.

I looked into the main room, where embers still glowed in the hearth, soothing and necessary. Fire could look so harmless and be so deadly.

The wind surged. I leaned my head on Mae's shoulder. "Do you smell smoke outside?"

"No," said Mae.

"No," said Birdie. "And even if you do, don't

forget, Willodeen, that not all wildfires are started by people. Sometimes they're nature's way of cleaning out a forest to make room for new growth."

"I didn't know that," I admitted.

"That's something you might learn more about, if you went to school now and again," Mae said.

I groaned, and Mae held up her palms. "Just a thought."

"Keep in mind that while we may seem like bottomless fonts of knowledge," said Birdie with a wry smile, "even Mae and I have our limitations." She nodded at Quinby. "With our screecher friend, for example, I'm afraid we haven't been of much use to you."

As clouds moved past the moon, Quinby shifted. She tilted her head back, mouth open, and for a moment I thought she was going to attempt an actual screech.

But no. It was just a yawn.

"What do you think will happen to Quinby?" I asked.

Again, I received no answers. Just wistful smiles and warm hugs.

"Whatever happens, we'll be there to help you, Willodeen," Mae said. "We love you more than life itself, do you understand that?"

I knew I should have said something then. "Thank you"? "I love you, too"?

Instead I just stroked Duuzuu and gave a quick nod.

"Do you want us to stay until you fall asleep?" Birdie asked.

"No, thanks," I said. "I have Duuzuu and Quinby." I sniffed the air. "You're sure you don't smell smoke?"

"I smell screecher," Birdie replied. "And that is all I smell."

I attempted a smile. "'When screechers were invented, Mother Nature made them scented,'" I said. "Connor made that up."

"He seems like a good friend," Mae said, and then she kissed my forehead.

Was he a friend? Had I made an actual friend? Me, against all odds?

After they left, I stared at Quinby, sitting there, obedient as a pet dog. As out of place as I sometimes felt, how must she feel?

"Why are you here, Quinby?" I asked.

She replied with a snort, and I laughed in spite of myself. "Whatever am I going to do with you?"

Another snort.

I sighed. If the unthinkable could happen, if your family could vanish in a moment, why couldn't a sculpture of a screecher come to life?

If horrible things were possible, why not magical ones?

I closed my eyes, but I knew sleep would not be coming, not when I could still hear the angry wind. Not when I'd seen the places dreams could take me.

THIRTY-ONE

The next day, Connor had to help his father with more setup for the Faire, then attend an afternoon council meeting. After I'd done my morning chores, I put Quinby in her harness, attached the rope, and loaded her into the wheelbarrow.

"Quiet, girl," I warned, covering her with the tarp. By now she knew the wheelbarrow meant an adventure—an adventure involving food—and she settled quickly. With Duuzuu on my shoulder, I headed toward the top of the ridge. I wanted to spend as much time as I could at the grove before word got out about the hummingbears.

I wasn't sure why. Maybe it was just that ornery part of me making trouble again. Maybe it was because the stand of blue willows had become a special place for Connor and me, one I didn't want to share—even though I knew I had to.

This afternoon, I promised myself, I would tell everyone about the hummingbears, no matter what.

I thought I could manage the wheelbarrow without Connor. But I was sadly mistaken. It took all my strength to make it up the hill, and I stopped several times to rest. With every pause, Quinby popped out her head to greet the world.

When we finally reached the hidden grove, I tied Quinby's rope around a blue willow trunk. Good thing Pa had taught me how to make a nice, solid knot when I was still young.

Sweet coos drifted down. Shading my eyes, I looked up to see not three, but seven hummingbears, each in a bubble nest. They now occupied two separate blue willows. The bubbles gleamed, slivering the sun like prisms.

The hummingbears looked completely at home. Three of them were dozing. Two were grooming themselves. The other two were looking down at me, Duuzuu, and Quinby with intense curiosity.

Quinby went to work digging for her meal at one of her two favorite trees while I retrieved my notebook from my pouch.

What was I looking for? What was I hoping to learn that I didn't already know?

I pulled off a couple blue willow twirls and gave them to Duuzuu. He ate one whole. Then he chewed the next one slowly and produced a perfect bubble.

Meanwhile, Quinby excavated with an energy that was almost frightening. But that was, of course, her job. To stay alive. To be what she was meant to be.

Poor Duuzuu would never be that lucky. He couldn't ever be totally free, completely himself. Could Quinby?

For the next hour, I counted. I sorted. I noted. I sketched. I measured.

Mostly, I wondered. Sometimes I simply wondered what I was wondering about.

Connor was right. We were doing the same thing: putting puzzle pieces together. He looked at nature and made art from it. I looked at nature and made sense of it. Tried to, anyway.

Sunlight filtered through the trees. The air warmed. The wind picked up, angry and edgy. By now, Quinby had dug in several spots. But she'd focused almost all her energy on holes near the two willows closest to the stream—the same trees where the humming-bears were nesting.

I felt the soil near one of her holes. It was slightly damp. Soft dirt meant easier digging—at least, it did if you had screecher claws. And she was still finding plenty of peacock snails. In fact, the deeper the hole, the more snails she seemed to uncover.

But why had the hummingbears chosen the same two trees for nesting? Because they were a bit closer to the water? Humming-bears weren't diggers. They wouldn't care if the soil was more porous.

I examined the leaves on each of the five willows. They were in full autumn attire: vivid blue on one side, shiny silver on the other, twisting like ribbons on an enormous gift. I removed a leaf from each tree and laid them side by side, held down by stones to keep them from blowing away.

Strange, the way hummingbears were so

particular about what they ate and where they nested. A lot of creatures were more open-minded, it seemed to me. Take screechers. They nested wherever they could. And even picky Quinby had learned to eat more than just peacock snails.

I thought of my brother, Toby. When he was one and a half, he'd refused to eat anything but porridge for months on end. I remembered Ma groaning *Give me strength* as Toby turned up his nose at anything but lumpy porridge. (The more lumps, the better.)

It seemed like a bad idea, all things considered. If you were open to eating lots of different things, wouldn't that make your life easier? If you could nest anywhere, didn't that give you more chances to find a safe resting place?

Pieces upon pieces, questions upon questions.

I was getting nowhere.

I gathered up my leaf samples and placed them in my notebook, labeled with numbers from one to five. I wasn't sure what I'd do with them. I could always give them to Duuzuu for a snack, although we tried to keep a good supply on hand.

By the time we departed, Duuzuu had made three impressive bubbles, and Quinby was giddily full.

I seemed to be the only one who left feeling disappointed.

CHAPTER

THIRTY-TWO

I dropped Duuzuu and Quinby off at the cottage. Mae and Birdie were napping in their rockers. They looked so fragile, almost childlike. Gently, I covered them both with quilts.

I chopped several logs, cleaned the hen-house, and swept the front porch. Then I grabbed a trowel, tucked it into my waist-pouch with my notebook, and headed down to the village.

The meeting was still in session. I could hear the villagers talking—or was it arguing?

Peeking around the half-open front door, I caught a glimpse of Connor. He was sitting in his usual spot, sketching, while a red-faced man droned on and on.

I waited, hoping Connor might look over and see me, but he seemed to be lost in another world.

Down by the riverwalk, the willow leaves tangled in the fitful wind. Still no humming-bears. Clouds scudded through the pale sky.

I took a deep breath. Was that smoke? Would I be asking that same question for the rest of my life?

I took out my trowel and walked past each blue willow. Every now and then, I poked into the soil at the base of a trunk. I'd never before tried digging for snails there, but almost every time, I found some. More, in fact, than I'd ever seen. Entire villages of them.

How Quinby would love to come here, I thought with a rueful smile. Of course, she couldn't. She'd be killed for the bounty. Or chased off, at the very least.

I pulled a few leaves from several trees, ignoring the strange looks I got from passersby. Then I made my way to the hillside where the new grove of blue willows had been planted, the ones Connor's father had said needed more water.

Sure enough, they seemed stunted and dry. I collected leaves from them, too.

On my way back to the cottage, I took samples of leaves from other kinds of trees. Oaks and purple maples, bitternuts and striped elms.

Mae and Birdie were still napping when I returned. Quinby greeted me with a polite snuffle. I checked my bed, where Duuzuu was dozing on my pillow. His three bubbles lay nearby, stuck together in the form of a triangle. A new bubble, still separate from the others, sat next to his right paw.

It made me happy that he'd taken up bubble-blowing again, something he would be doing in the wild.

It was also quite convenient since I needed to borrow a bubble.

Returning to the kitchen, I pulled a sheet of paper from my notebook and tore it into pieces. On each scrap of paper, I wrote a number and location. *Hidden Grove 1. Hidden Grove 2, 3, 4, and 5.*

I took my samples from the riverside willows, the new blue willow grove, and the leaves I'd collected from random trees. One by one, I laid them out on the kitchen table. Below them, I placed my five leaf samples from the hidden grove.

Tiptoeing back to my bedside, I picked up Duuzuu's single bubble.

Fortunately, he was a sound sleeper.

I felt a tad guilty borrowing his creation. But I knew he could always make more bubbles.

Back at the table, I started with the five river-bank willow leaf samples. I touched Duuzuu's bubble to the first leaf.

The bubble and the leaf should have stuck together instantly. They didn't.

Same thing with the other four leaves.

Next I tried the new willow grove samples. The bubble slid right off every leaf.

I followed with leaves from the other types of trees. The same thing happened. That didn't surprise me. Pa had told me that bubble nests only stuck to blue willow leaves. Still, I wanted to be sure.

It was time for the hidden grove samples. Leaf one, leaf two, leaf three: nothing. The bubble refused to attach.

I was down to two more leaves. Numbers four and five were from Quinby's preferred trees, where she did almost all her digging.

The trees where the seven hummingbear nests were situated.

Gently I touched the bubble to leaf four. The bubble stuck. It was like fitting the right key into a stubborn lock.

I moved the bubble, now trailing a leaf, to hidden grove leaf five. Once again, the leaf adhered. And once again, I could not separate bubble from leaf.

I stared at the table, covered with leaves and scraps of paper. I grinned. Then I got out my notebook, and I began to write as fast as my pencil would let me.

I wrote the same way Quinby had dug that morning: hungrily, with a sense of purpose. As if I was doing what I was meant to do.

THIRTY-THREE

When I was done with my notes, I ran back to the village. I had to tell someone, and that someone was Connor. More than anyone, he would appreciate how I'd puzzled something through. How I might even have an answer to the village's hummingbear problem.

Near the bottom of the hill, I saw Miss Rossit, the teacher, talking to Connor's father. "Hello, Willodeen," she said.

I was surprised she remembered me. It had been ages since I'd been to school.

"You certainly look excited," said Mr. Burke.

"I figured something out!" I exclaimed. "Something . . . well, I think it might be really important."

No sooner were the words out of my mouth than I could feel my face flushing. I looked down at the ground, instantly self-conscious.

"Can you tell us more?" asked Miss Rossit.

I started to answer, but when I looked back up at Miss Rossit, her smile had faded to a look of alarm.

The wind had kicked up yet again. And with it came an unmistakable smell.

"Smoke," she said, but of course, I already knew.

I checked the hills, trying to place the fire. "Up there."

I pointed to Roundtop Ridge, where the

train tracks were. The same place the last big fire had started.

Another strong gust, and the fire burst into life.

It was beautiful in its fury.

The billowing gray smoke, with its eddies and swirls.

The red flood of flames, moving slowly toward the village.

The sparks and embers, popping and fading like fireflies.

I gulped, trying to quell the panic in my chest.

"My mother and baby are at home," said Miss Rossit, wringing her hands. "I've got to check on them. Will you be all right, Willodeen?"

"Yes."

"I think Connor's down by the river. I need to find him." Mr. Burke gripped my shoulders. "Be careful, Willodeen."

"I will."

Around us, villagers moved purposefully. Some ran toward the river, carrying buckets. Others had shovels and hoes. Despite the quickening flames, a calm determination filled the air.

After all, we'd been through this before.

I'd been through this before.

The searing burns on my feet. My lungs, scraped raw. The screams of my family.

I needed to run. To hide. But where could I possibly be safe?

And then it hit me.

I didn't want to run away. I wanted to run *toward*.

Birdie. Mae.

Duuzuu. Quinby.

I had no time to waste.

Spinning around, I raced back up the hill to the cottage, to the place where everything I needed and loved could be found.

To my home.

CHAPTER

THIRTY-FOUR

By the time I neared the cottage, Mae and Birdie were already heading down the road, calling for me.

"Willodeen!" Birdie cried as she and Mae wrapped me in their arms.

I wiped my stinging eyes and pointed to Birdie's feet. "You're only wearing one shoe!"

"As soon as we smelled the smoke, we dashed out the door," Mae said, and I couldn't tell if she was laughing or crying. "We weren't sure where you were."

"It doesn't matter now," said Birdie. "We're all here. We're all safe." She nodded toward Roundtop Ridge. "Same place as last time. It's moving slowly, though, and veering east a bit. The cottage will probably be fine, unless the wind changes. Still, I'm worried sick about the folks over that way . . ."

I heard a frantic cooing sound and turned to see Duuzuu, half fluttering, half running toward me.

"Duuzuu!" I said, and he landed on my shoulder, rubbing his head against my neck.

"Oh my!" Mae slapped a hand to her cheek. "The door. We left it open!"

We all thought it. But no one said it.

Quinby.

I ran back to the cottage, with Duuzuu hanging on for dear life. Mae and Birdie trailed behind.

The front gate was wide open. So was the cottage door.

"Quinby!" I yelled, my pulse hammering. "Quinby!"

Her box was empty. The cottage was deserted.

We checked the yard, the shed, every hiding place we could think of.

"She's gone." I whispered it. I suppose I figured if I said it quietly enough, it might not be true.

"She's probably just hiding in the woods," said Mae, but I could hear the uncertainty in her voice. "I'm so sorry, love. All we could think of was getting to you."

I patted Mae's back. "It's not your fault."

"Maybe," said Birdie, "she went up to the grove where you and Connor go."

"Connor!" I said. "Mr. Burke was looking for him."

My heart was tearing apart like a piece of wet paper.

I wanted to protect Mae and Birdie and Duuzuu.

I wanted to find Quinby.

And I wanted to be sure that Connor was safe.

"I'm going back down to the village," I said. "I have to see if Connor is all right."

"You can't—" Mae began, but I cut her off.

"I'll need water buckets," I said. "You two stay here with Duuzuu. Keep an eye out for Quinby, in case she comes back."

Birdie and Mae exchanged a look that spoke volumes. I was the child, and they were the adults. But I was also healthy and able-bodied, and they were not.

I could see they wanted to stop me. And I could see they weren't going to.

"If I can help, I want to try," I said.

They both nodded.

"I'll come straight back here to fetch you if the fire changes course," I promised.

"Take the buckets on the front porch," said Birdie. I'd never before heard her voice tremble.

I set Duuzuu on a chair and gave Mae and Birdie a quick hug.

Four buckets were right outside the door. I grabbed two and left two for Mae and Birdie, hoping against hope they wouldn't need them.

I didn't let myself say the words until I'd reached the front gate.

"I love you," I called.

THIRTY-FIVE

Smoke hung in the village like a menacing fog. The air was yellow-gray. It hurt to breathe.

I started at the riverfront. No Connor.

I tried the village hall. Again, nothing.

No doubt his father had found him. Connor was probably fine. And yet I couldn't stop thinking, *What if? What if?*

Near the carousel, a bucket brigade was hard at work. A long line of villagers snaked from the fountain to the edge of the woods, where the fire appeared to be heading. The first person in line scooped out water into pails, pots, and buckets, then passed it down. Meanwhile, two other groups dug trenches and cleared brush on the hillside, hoping to contain the fire's spread.

Practically every resident seemed to be there. People were sweating and panting, their faces smudged with soot, their cheeks marked with tears.

I walked down the line, choking and coughing like everyone else, and finally, there he was.

When Connor saw me, his grin practically overtook his whole face. "Willodeen!" he cried as he passed a metal pail to the woman beside him. "My father said he saw you, but I was still worried." He wiped his brow with the back of his hand. "Really worried."

"Everyone's fine," I said. I paused. "Except Quinby. She's disappeared, Connor. Vanished."

His face fell. "You're . . . sure?"

"I'm sure."

I wanted to say more, but it wasn't the right time.

I took my buckets to the fountain, headed to the end of the line, and joined my neighbors in their fight. Our fight.

We worked together for hours. After the fountain ran dry, we took turns hauling water from the river. When the wind picked up, we covered our faces with handkerchiefs and bandannas. When our hands blistered from the buckets and shovels, we tied scraps of cloth around our palms.

We helped each other because we were all we had.

Because we knew that against the brutal, timeless forces of nature, the best we could hope for was a truce.

CHAPTER
THIRTY-SIX

By midnight, the wind had calmed, and flames had faded to a swath of glowing embers. Against the full-moon sky, skeletons of burnt trees marked the fire's path.

A few buildings were damaged. But except for some blistered hands, stinging eyes, and lingering coughs, no one was badly hurt.

It was, we all knew, a miracle.

Connor and I agreed to meet the next morning. Exhausted as we were, neither of us slept well. As dawn broke, we were already searching for Quinby. We brought Duuzuu, on the off chance his presence might draw her out.

Naturally, we started in the hidden grove, since it was our best hope. There was no sign of her, although the number of bubble nests had grown to eleven.

Connor gazed up at the nests. "Eleven," he marveled. "I wish I understood why they keep coming here."

"Actually, I think I may have figured it out," I said.

Connor's mouth dropped open. "What?" he cried. "Why didn't you tell me?"

"I was about to yesterday. Then the fire came, and what with losing Quinby and all . . ." I'd been so thrilled about my discovery, but without Quinby there, everything felt hollow.

"Willodeen," said Connor, "this is important. Please. Tell me."

I motioned him over to the two willows where Quinby had spent most of her time digging.

"Well . . ." It was hard to know where to start. "First, I had to figure out the right question to ask. Why are the hummingbears only nesting here? What makes these two trees so special?"

"Good question."

"Think about when we started seeing fewer hummingbears migrating to the village, Connor." Now that I was explaining my ideas, I felt my initial excitement returning. "It was around the same time the village council decided to put a bounty on screechers, right?"

Connor sat on a rock, hand in his chin, listening intently. "That could easily just be coincidence, though."

I held up an index finger. "Maybe. But is it also a coincidence that hummingbears are nesting here, where Quinby's been eating, and nowhere else?"

I knelt next to one of the two deep holes Quinby had created. "I wish I had my trowel," I said. "Better yet, I wish I had Quinby."

Reaching down past my elbow, I managed to grab a handful of snails.

"Look," I said. "The farther down you dig, the more snails you find. That's why Quinby kept returning to the same holes. She found hundreds of snails here, Connor. Maybe more."

"And ate them all," he joked.

I returned the snails and brushed my dirty hands on my coat. "I started to wonder. What makes these two trees, and only these two, attractive to the hummingbears? Could it be because Quinby has eaten so many of the snails near their roots? Maybe having too many snails changes the trees in some important way."

"Too many?" Connor frowned.

I stood. "Nature likes things in balance. My pa taught me that. Maybe the screechers kept the snail population in check."

Connor did not look convinced.

"So to test my idea," I said, "I . . . I conducted an experiment, I guess you'd say. I got a bunch of different leaves, including samples from these blue willows, the ones down by the riverfront, and the new grove. To be thorough, I added some other trees, too." I stopped long enough to cough. My throat still burned from yesterday's smoke. "Then I . . . um, borrowed . . . one of Duuzuu's bubbles."

"A bubble? Why?"

"Just a hunch. Luck, I s'pose. I figured there had to be something special about these two trees. Something connected to having fewer snails around. It could have been, I don't know, the way the leaves taste. Or the strength

of the branches. It could have been anything."
I lifted my shoulders. "But since I happened to
have a bubble, I started there."

Connor cocked his head. "And?"

"And the bubbles wouldn't stick, Connor!
Not to any of the other blue willow leaves. Not
to any of the other tree leaves. Just to the leaves
from these two trees!"

I paused to catch my breath. I felt buzzy
and hopeful. Even confident.

Connor stared up at the nests overhead.
"That has to be it, Willodeen."

"I still don't understand what the reason is,"
I added. "Do the snails harm the roots? Does
that affect the sap in the leaves? But if I'm
right, we might fix things by luring screechers
back to Perchance. They could keep the snails
from getting out of control."

Connor shook his head. "You are amazing.
Do you realize that?"

I shrugged. "I feel like Quinby showed me the answer to the puzzle," I said, sighing. "And now she's gone."

"*You* found the answer, Willodeen," Connor replied with a sad smile. "Quinby just provided the appetite."

THIRTY-SEVEN

When we returned to town, the sour smell of smoke hung over everything. The councillors had hastily scheduled a council meeting to discuss fire damage and consider the future. Many people blamed the railroad for causing the fire, but the dry conditions and Dragon Sighs clearly had played a part in it, too.

In any case, I knew what I had to do.

Connor and I walked to the carousel. Like much of the village, it was coated in ash.

I sat on the blue unicorn, and Connor leaned on my favorite gold spotted pony. "Do you think we'll ever see Quinby again?" I asked, stifling another cough. Birdie and Mae had given me a foul-tasting elixir that morning to soothe my throat.

Connor stroked Duuzuu, who was perched on his shoulder. "Do you want an honest answer, Willodeen? Or do you want me to lie?"

"Lying would be nice. But tell me the truth."

"I doubt we'll ever see her again."

I wiped away a tear.

"But whatever she was, wherever she is, it's a good thing we had her here with us for a while."

"It never would have happened if you hadn't given me that puzzler."

Connor shook his head. "We don't know that."

"Well, it was certainly quite a coincidence."

People were already streaming into the hall for the council meeting. It looked like the entire village had shown up: men and women, old and young. To my surprise, I saw Birdie and Mae slowly climbing the steps. I called out, and they both waved.

"You know, school will be starting up again soon," Connor said.

"I know."

"It's not so bad, really." Connor wiped some ash off the gold pony's mane. "'Course, it'd be better with you there," he added, avoiding my gaze.

"I really don't like crowds," I reminded him. "Or"—I grinned—"you know: people."

"But you do like learning."

"True," I admitted. "Birdie and Mae say it's up to me. They seem to think I'm too stubborn to argue with."

"You? Stubborn?" Connor teased. "My father

229

says I don't have a choice. He's sort of the opposite of Birdie and Mae."

"He just wants what's best for you, I think. The worry on his face yesterday, when he didn't know where you were . . . He loves you so much."

"I know." Connor reached up to scratch Duuzuu's ear.

"All that worrying. Seems like the worst part of being an adult to me."

"Not to mention all those meetings." Connor grinned. "I suppose it'll be our turn, soon enough." He pointed to the hall. A few stragglers were still arriving. "You ready?"

I hopped off the unicorn. "You know," I said, surprising myself, "I think I am."

THIRTY-EIGHT

By the time Thaddeus Vilner slammed down his gavel, the room was packed.

"Yesterday," he said, his voice solemn, "we saw the best of ourselves. Working to fight a common enemy. Caring for each other." His voice cracked. "We've fought other fires, faced other problems. But this time we worked together in a way I've never seen before."

The crowd murmured and nodded.

"My grandmother, rest her soul," continued Thaddeus, "had a saying." He paused to blow his nose. "'Thaddie,' she would say—she called me Thaddie even when I was a grown man—'Thaddie, with enough whispers, you can make a roar.' Yesterday, our beloved village of Perchance managed to roar."

The mood was different from the last meeting I'd attended. Villagers stood in a long line, waiting for their chance to speak, but they were patient and kind to each other. I heard plenty of worry and fear. I saw some tears and even heard some laughter.

But the fresh experience of yet another fire seemed to have left most people feeling grateful and humbled.

Everything and anything was discussed. Clearing the land near the railroad tracks. Creating a volunteer fire brigade. Planting trees that resisted burning and didn't require too much water.

It wasn't just the fires. People talked about building a new school. About recruiting a doctor to live in the town. About building and growing and improving.

And almost everyone talked about the Faire. Would it happen? Had anyone seen more hummingbears? Was there any hope at all?

I stood at the very back of the line—the last to speak, and the youngest—and waited my turn. When Thaddeus saw me, he groaned.

"Ahh," he said, "would this be about the screechers, yet again? We have an awful lot to think about, as you can see, my dear. Perhaps another time."

I blinked, flustered. "This will only take a minute," I said.

"We're all weary," said Thaddeus as a baby wailed. "And the little ones are restless. We've no time to talk about those smelly monsters of yours."

Connor stood. "Sir," he said loudly, "you'll

want to hear what Willodeen has to say. Trust me. We all need to hear it."

Thaddeus narrowed his eyes. "The chair didn't recognize you, boy." He waved his gavel, ready to adjourn, but Connor's father held up a warning hand.

"Thaddeus," he said, "give Willodeen a chance."

Miss Rossit nodded. "Yes," she said. "Goodness knows we've heard plenty from all the adults."

Thaddeus considered. After a moment, he slumped in his chair. "Fine," he said, dropping his gavel on the table. "Speak your piece."

And so I did.

I told everyone what I'd observed.

I told them about the hidden grove.

About a screecher who dined on peacock snails. (I did not tell them how she'd come into my life.)

About the eleven hummingbear nests that Connor and I had discovered.

When I mentioned the nests, the entire room burst into applause. People hugged and cheered and raised their fists. I looked over at Connor and we shared a smile.

After the group calmed down, I explained, best as I could, how screechers and hummingbears and blue willows all needed each other, even if it wasn't easy for us to see or understand.

I said they were a community, same as we were.

At this, some people stirred. I heard murmurs, shifting in seats, sighs.

"The same as us?" someone demanded.

I noticed a gray-templed man, nattily dressed, standing to my left. I'd seen him before. It was James McLachlan, owner of the nearby mill. "Are you actually suggesting, child, that a foul beast deserves the same regard as a human being?" he asked.

"He's right! We aren't animals!" a woman yelled, and others muttered their agreement.

I gulped. I knew what was in my heart. But turning that into words—coherent, grown-up words—perhaps that was more than I could manage.

Behind me, I heard others standing. More angry folks, no doubt.

Was this how screechers felt? Cornered? Outnumbered?

"'One touch of nature makes the whole world kin.'"

I spun around. It was Mae. Declaiming with all her theatrical flair.

"That's Shakespeare," she added. "In case you were wondering."

Birdie stood, too. "Let Willodeen speak," she said. It wasn't a request. It was a demand. "And be sure you listen."

Never had she seemed taller, or more invincible.

The room fell silent, shocked, no doubt, by the audacity of these two old women.

I was shaking from head to toe.

I took a breath.

I found my voice.

I said that we were all connected. People and plants and fish and birds and yes, even screechers.

I told everyone that it would take time and work to undo what we'd done.

That even if we brought screechers back, nothing would change overnight.

That we probably wouldn't have much of a Faire this year. Maybe even for many years.

And then I told them one last thing. I told them that nature knows more than we do. And she probably always will.

CHAPTER

THIRTY-NINE

When the meeting ended, Connor and I led a group of villagers, including all the councillors, to the hidden grove. Another nest had already been added in our brief absence.

It felt odd, having all those people crowded into the space where Connor and I had spent so much time. But the joy on their faces made it all worthwhile. Several people openly wept at the sight of those miraculous nests and their gentle residents.

Connor walked me back home. We didn't talk at all. We didn't need to.

I'd just waved goodbye to him from the front door of the cottage when he shouted, "Wait, Willodeen!"

I returned to the gate. "What's wrong?"

He pointed to his shoulder. "You almost forgot something!"

Duuzuu was curled in a tight ball, dozing away. He might as well have been cuddled on my pillow. Connor ran his index finger along the hummingbear's back. Duuzuu opened one eye, then closed it.

"He's snoring," I pointed out.

Connor smiled.

"He only snores when he feels safe," I said.

"Wake up, Duuzuu," said Connor. "It's time to go home."

"No." I took a step back and shook my head. "I think . . . I think I want you to take him, Connor. Let's face it, he much prefers your company."

My words hung in the air. I hadn't realized I was going to say them.

Was I making a terrible mistake? Giving a gift was almost as bad as accepting one. It made you obliged. It created a connection.

Still. Connor had given me Quinby, in a way. And Duuzuu adored Connor. It only seemed fair.

I stroked Duuzuu. "Do you want to stay with Connor?" I asked.

Duuzuu yawned, glancing at us both with heavy-lidded eyes. He replied with a firm coo.

"Was that yes, no, or maybe?" I asked Connor.

"Actually, it was a yes."

"Of course it was."

I made myself look Connor in the eyes. I saw gratitude there.

But I didn't feel beholden. I didn't feel weighed down. I just felt glad.

"You're sure?" he asked.

"I'll see you both plenty," I said, and suddenly I realized that might actually be true.

CHAPTER
FORTY

That night, I couldn't sleep. I missed the soothing snores of Duuzuu and Quinby.

I closed my eyes. I saw fire raging. Smoke without end. Forests forever changed.

I opened my eyes. Moon. Shoes. Notebooks. Ceiling.

I closed my eyes again. I saw the hidden grove. I saw adults listening to a child. To me.

Eyes open. Quinby's box sat empty. Duuzuu's spot was cold and bare.

Once more, I closed my eyes. I saw Duu-zuu asleep on Connor's pillow, dreaming of a world where he could still slip through the clouds.

I smiled.

And then I fell asleep.

Part Five

CHAPTER
FORTY-ONE

We had no Faire that year.

Everyone reluctantly agreed that allowing tourists to visit those precious nests in the hidden grove would be too dangerous. We didn't want to disturb the few hummingbears who'd returned.

The council created a committee to decide the best way forward. It consisted of four adult members, including Miss Rossit and Mr. Burke.

And one junior member. Me.

I barely said a word at the first committee meeting. But when I realized the adults actually wanted to hear my thoughts, I relaxed. Soon I began to realize how complicated every decision we made was going to be. How would it affect the villagers? The land? The river? Birds and insects and animals?

To begin with, we stopped the bounty on screechers. That much was easy.

We considered paying villagers to remove the peacock snails that were harming our willows. But when folks tried, they ended up damaging the tree roots. Screechers were simply much better at it.

Some people suggested poisoning the snails, and the committee thought about it briefly. But Miss Rossit and I both agreed that we might end up killing the trees in the process, not to mention other creatures.

When we learned about a nearby village that

had been overrun with screechers, we created a new incentive for hunters. A payment for every screecher from that area, safely trapped and brought to Perchance, alive and well.

It wasn't perfect. We risked disrupting screecher families. But it was a compromise we felt we could live with. And bringing in screechers would help keep the snail population under control.

It helped that nature is resilient, and sometimes surprisingly quick to recover. The screechers resettled easily. And by the next autumn, a quarter of the riverside blue willows had hummingbear nests in them.

When tourists complained about the horrible beasts stinking up our village, we learned to simply shrug and say, "When screechers were invented, Mother Nature made them scented."

That fall's Faire, despite having fewer hummingbears, was just like it had always been.

Performers lined the streets. The inns were completely full. Music played for days.

I went a few times, though I tried to keep my distance, for the most part. I still hated noise and crowds. That certainly hadn't changed. Nevertheless, I'd managed to start attending school again, with the eager support of Miss Rossit and Connor.

To be honest, I missed a few days now and then.

Sometimes I just needed to wander the woods. Being close to nature gave my heart a chance to heal.

I s'pose I'll be healing till the end of my days. Seems that's how it goes, when you lose someone you love.

All things considered, school wasn't so bad. Miss Rossit obtained two books just for me. One about zoology, the study of animals. The other about botany, the science of plants. And those always brought me back.

Those books. And Connor.

The last day of the Faire, I promised to help Connor close up his stand. He still sold hummingbears, but he'd started making other puzzlers, too. They were wonderfully strange. Hawks with fins. Lions with wings. Screechers with smiles.

His father admitted he didn't understand what they were. Or why Connor wanted to make them. But he didn't stand in Connor's way, either.

Some folks sneered when they saw Connor's puzzlers. On the first day of the Faire, while Mr. Burke, Connor, and I were chatting, a woman walked past Connor's stand and loudly whispered, "What on earth is wrong with that boy?"

To our shock, Mr. Burke responded, "What on earth is wrong with your imagination?"

Connor and I had to kneel behind the stand to hide our laughter.

That final eve, after I helped Connor pack up his things, we joined Mae and Birdie at the riverwalk. The sun was melting onto Roundtop Ridge, a puddle of pinks and reds and violets, and the bubble nests mirrored the spectacle.

Duuzuu, sitting on Connor's shoulder, cooed at the other hummingbears.

"Was that yes, no, or maybe, Connor?" Mae asked, wrapping her shawl around her shoulders.

"I've never heard that particular coo," said

Connor. "Maybe that was just between Duu-zuu and them."

We passed a juggler and a man playing a sweetly sad song on a mandolin. When we reached Nedwit Poole's stand, Connor used the money he'd made that day to buy each of us one of the baker's hummingbear-shaped pastries.

"You shouldn't waste your coins on us, Connor," said Birdie.

"Bird's right," Mae agreed, although she was already wiping berry filling from her chin. "As a matter of fact, I sold three shawls today."

"It's good to have the Faire return." Birdie leaned back her head and smiled at the nests above us. "Wouldn't have happened without you, Willodeen."

I grinned. "Piffle," I said, and we all laughed.

We sauntered along the rest of the river-walk. "Connor," I said, "do you remember how you told me you were writing a story about Quinby?"

He nodded.

"Did you ever finish it?"

"I'm getting close to the end," he said. "I have the feeling there's just one more part I need to add."

"I'd like to read it when you're ready."

"You will. I promise." He smiled. "As soon as I puzzle out the rest."

We walked Mae and Birdie home. With their permission—and a large lantern—Connor and I decided to walk up to the hidden grove.

"Be careful," Mae warned. "And don't stay too long."

"I promise," I told her, and I kissed her cheek.

"Screecher hunting, are you?" Birdie asked.

"Just looking for more questions," I replied.

Birdie laughed. "Trust me, Willodeen. You'll never run out of those."

The screecher has come back to the place where she began.

Some of the awkward animals, the ones with their two-legged lurching and their odd smell, brought her back. There was a net, screaming, scrabbling. But no pain.

They'd put her in a dark box, and after a while, they'd let her go in these woods.

Such strange animals! Even now, she isn't sure whether to trust or fear them.

She knows this place well. Already she's found her old feeding spot, the stream with its cold, sweet water. And the trees, their roots dotted with the snails that make her drool. It's always good to eat, but oh, those snails! Is there anything better?

She inhales the scents of the village, the river, the forest, the blue willows. The faint smell of smoke from a fire, long past, still lingers. But more than anything, the air is full of life, messy and urgent and thrilling.

Night is coming, and she's pleased with the abandoned den she's found. Cozy, warm, it's protected on three sides.

Why was she brought back to this place, with its ferns and snails and singing stream? What purpose is she supposed to serve?

She knows only that she is glad to be here.

Drifting off, the screecher settles into her den. But something new is coming! She jerks awake, alert to fresh scents and sounds.

She hears the grunts and sighs and songs of the awkward animals, which sometimes, but not always, means danger.

She tests the air.

She knows those two scents. She remembers those sounds.

They mean gentle hands and warm food and
safe sleep.

Another scent floats on the breeze. She recalls
a furry, winged animal with wide eyes, ever
watchful.

She waits. The movement has stopped, but the scents remain.

Could they be hiding? Observing her from a safe distance?

She makes the night noise from long ago, a grumbly purr from deep within her chest.

A moment later, there it is: a delicate, answering trill.

After low clouds, the moon makes its appearance. The forest floor shimmers.

She sits up. She raises her head. Above the treetops, stars blossom.

The sound she makes is wild and loud and free.

It hurts, it's so loud.

She screeches again. What a lovely sound it is!

She's not sure why she needs to do it. Who knows why we do what we do?

There are so many questions that will never have answers. But she is certain of one thing.

She has just a moment on this old, wise earth, this earth that will always be wiser than its inhabitants. And she is lucky indeed to be part of its magic.

ACKNOWLEDGMENTS

My endless gratitude to these remarkable folks
at Feiwel & Friends/Macmillan:

- Rich Deas, senior creative director;
- Starr Baer, associate copy chief;
- Bethany Reis, copy editor;
- the MCPG marketing and publicity team,
  especially Mary Van Akin and Melissa Zar;
- the all-star sales team.

Special thanks and an extra-loud screech to:

- Jean Feiwel, publisher par excellence,
  who helped me get my start many years

ago, and has been providing guidance and insight ever since;

- Charles Santoso, *Willodeen*'s breathtakingly brilliant illustrator;
- Elena Giovinazzo, my agent, relentless champion and the best in the biz, and everyone at Pippin Properties;
- Mary Cate Stevenson and Noah Nofz at Two Cats Communications, for their invaluable help and good humor.

And finally . . .

- To booksellers, teachers, librarians: You are heroes, in so many ways. Thank you for your tireless work connecting readers and books;
- To Liz Szabla, editor without peer, whose special brand of encouragement and flawless instincts made this book possible:

There are no words to thank you, dear editor and dear friend;

- To my friends and family—especially Julia, Clara, and Michael: I'm so grateful for you all;
- And to young environmental activists everywhere: We thank you. We need you. Never stop fighting. And never stop hoping.

Thank you for reading this Feiwel & Friends book. The friends who made *Willodeen* possible are:

Jean Feiwel, Publisher
Liz Szabla, Associate Publisher
Rich Deas, Senior Creative Director
Holly West, Senior Editor
Anna Roberto, Senior Editor
Kat Brzozowski, Senior Editor
Dawn Ryan, Executive Managing Editor
Kim Waymer, Senior Production Manager
Erin Siu, Associate Editor
Emily Settle, Associate Editor
Foyinsi Adegbonmire, Associate Editor
Rachel Diebel, Assistant Editor
Michelle Gengaro, Designer
Starr Baer, Associate Copy Chief

Follow us on Facebook or visit us online at mackids.com. Our books are friends for life.